WINNING THE PLAYER

RULES OF THE GAME
BOOK 3

HEATHER YOUNG-NICHOLS

Winning the Player
Rules of the Game 3
USA Today Bestselling Author
Heather Young-Nichols

heatheryoungnichols.com

ALSO BY HEATHER YOUNG-NICHOLS

Bound by Magic

With Amelia J. Matthews

Dirt on the Diamond

After Office Hours: Seducing the Professor

CHAPTER 1
COBB

*S*weat ran down my neck because it was hot as fuck outside today. Fucking day games where we had to play under the heat lamp of a sun without an ounce of shade.

I wasn't complaining really. The team paid me a lot of money to play a damn game.

My catcher gave me a sign and I shook it off. I knew exactly what I wanted to throw this guy. If I was right, the game would be over. The catcher threw another and I shook that one off. He sighed then gave me the one that I wanted and I nodded.

I did my normal windup and released the ball.

It was the sweet sound of the last ball I pitched hitting the catcher's glove that I loved the most. The call of a strike right after was the second-best thing.

That was always true, but especially today when I'd pitched a complete game and we won.

Being on top felt amazing.

My catcher came out and patted me on the back as we fell into our after-win ritual with lots of congratulations and talk of how fucking amazing we were.

Sure, we had big egos but we were amazing. There was no point in denying it.

"You coming tonight?" the catcher, Peters, asked once we were in the clubhouse.

"Yup." Not that I wanted to.

I loved being on this team, loved living in New York. I wasn't necessarily into the *going out* portion, but most of the single guys on the team were going, so it felt required. I was at the top of my game. At twenty-three years old, I was one of the best pitchers in baseball right now. I was supposed to be living life to the fullest.

But I was the relationship guy. Of all my brothers, I tended to like to be in relationships more than being with random women. Though somehow I was single right now and two of my brothers had found their endgames. Surprised the hell out of me that Silas and Urban were in committed relationships. Don't get me wrong. I'd had my share of random hookups. Just not the rest of the world's share, like my brothers had. I wasn't desperate to be with someone, but I liked the comfort that came from it.

Since I didn't currently have a girlfriend, there wasn't an excuse that I deemed good enough to get out of tonight.

I'd go. Have a drink. Then head home at the earliest possible time. That was the plan. If I had a girl, maybe we would've stayed longer, but my last relationship had ended six months ago and no one had grabbed my interest since. I had a woman I slept with sometimes, when it worked out for both of us, kind of a *friends with benefits* situation, but I wouldn't take her to a party in this capacity and she wouldn't have wanted to go.

And that was how I found myself at this party, annoyed that I was there in the first place. I'd had my drink but was biding my time until it was acceptable for me to leave.

It wasn't exactly a work thing but close enough. I was a team player through and through, so I'd stay… as long as I had to.

"Hey, Cobb." This tall brunette who looked familiar but I couldn't place slid up to me, standing so that her breasts brushed against my chest.

"Hey." I gave her a head nod then grabbed a second beer. I wouldn't drink it, but I'd hold it, maybe take a few sips. It gave me something to do with my hands.

"Great party, right?" She looked up at me as she twirled a lock of hair around her finger.

"Sure." I knew this woman, but damn, I knew I'd seen her somewhere before.

"It's a little loud in here," she called out and that was an understatement. "Want to go somewhere… quieter?" She trailed the finger that she'd had her shiny hair wrapped around down my chest.

"I'm good," I called out to her.

She furrowed her brows. "I wasn't really saying to talk. I've wanted to get close to you for a while now."

Yeah, no shit. She wasn't being cryptic at all.

"I know what you meant." I took a step back. "I'm good here."

Her eyes narrowed. "Most guys don't turn me down."

Something about the way she'd said it didn't sit well in my stomach. "Then you should go find one of them." Then I walked away from her, thinking that this was the best time for me to make my exit.

On my way through the crowd, I'd just gotten

outside when Peters stopped me. His first name was Lucian and he would much rather go by his last name. He was tall and built like a brick house. Reminded me of my brother Brooks. He was massive even compared to the rest of us and we were pretty big guys in our own rights.

"You know who that was, right?" he asked, bringing me to a stop.

"Who?" I asked. He jerked his head in the direction I'd just come from. "Oh. No. No idea. But I'm heading out."

"That's Hannah." When the name didn't register with me he added, "Johnson. Doug Johnson's daughter."

Now that... I recognized.

Doug Johnson was the team owner and one rich son of a bitch. "OK. Well, I didn't do anything, so we're good." Because fucking with the team owner's daughter could get a guy in a lot of trouble. I couldn't imagine what would happen to a player if he fucked with my sister, Camden, and not just because my grandpa owned the team. She had four older brothers who were all currently playing this game professionally. We knew ballplayers and sure as hell didn't want one around our sister.

"Yeah... see..." He scratched at his jaw. "She's

got a bit of a reputation." I folded my arms over my chest and waited. Peters didn't come off as the kind of guy who'd judge a woman for doing the same shit men did, so I was going to give him the benefit of the doubt. "That she's vindictive. Doesn't take well to rejection."

I let my arms fall. Was that all? "I don't care if she takes it well or not. I wasn't an asshole, so…"

He shrugged. "I'm not sure that matters. Just… wanted you to know."

"Yeah. Thanks." Leaving the party was all I wanted to do right now and I wasn't going to give the owner's daughter another thought.

I'd been there, people had seen me, now it was time to retreat into the solitude of my own apartment.

A month later, I was stomping down the hallway near the clubhouse then burst through the door, letting the thing hit the wall behind it.

"What the fuck?" Peters called out. "You're going to hurt yourself on your starting day."

"I'm not starting," I spat as I tossed my bag into my locker.

"What? It's your day. You start every five days and we need you to start today. We're playing Los Angeles."

"I know. Talk to your skipper." That was the manager, also known as the coach, but in professional baseball, we didn't call him 'the coach.'

"What's going on?"

"Apparently, I have muscle strain."

He leaned back in his chair and looked me over. "You look fine to me. You're not limping, nursing an arm. What the fuck are you talking about?"

"I was just informed that I'm on the disabled list for muscle strain." He narrowed his eyes. "I'm benched, Peters. The only thing is, I don't know why." I slammed my fist into the back of my locker.

He hopped to his feet. "Don't do that. Your hands are valuable. Do you know what happens if you break one of them?"

I snorted. "I'll be benched on the DL?" Because that was exactly what had happened.

"Well, fuck." He sighed.

There wasn't anything else to say about it. I was benched, but no one had sacked up to tell me why. Since I wasn't hurt, this was a punishment for something, but who the fuck knew what.

That game, I had to be in the dugout in uniform and watch my team lose. The pitcher they replaced me with was great, but he was moved up a day in his rotation, so his arms hadn't gotten the rest they normally did. The other guys looked at me with questions in their eyes. Questions that I didn't have any answers to and thankfully, they didn't ask or I would've lost my shit where cameras were watching.

It wasn't just my reputation I was protecting but my family's. Playing this game when your family owned a team wasn't the easy nepo baby way into baseball that some thought it was. I had to work harder. Be better. Just to prove I should be there at all.

It wasn't until the next morning that anyone bothered to talk to me.

I was called up to the general manager's office. Waiting for me there was the GM and the owner of the team and no one else. Johnson, the owner, didn't interact with the players too much, but when I'd met him, he'd been a self-inflated asshole.

This wasn't a good sign.

"Thanks for coming up," the GM, Walter, said as soon as I was through the door. Like I had a choice.

"Yeah, of course." This was the business side of things and I had to act accordingly.

"You can have a seat," Doug said as he pointed to the chair. He was tall and thin with hair that was mostly gray and cut short. He looked exactly how you'd picture someone who'd worked in an office his whole life. There wasn't anything wrong with it, but he looked like an accountant.

So, I took the seat, though I thought that I'd rather have kept standing.

"You're out," Doug told me without even trying to finesse it.

I raised an eyebrow. "What?"

"You're out."

Walter sighed. "The decision has been made to cut you from the team." He shifted uncomfortably. "It was asked that Jason let us break the news to you."

So my agent knew and didn't tell me. Of course he did, but this was going to mean a conversation between the two of us. He worked for me and my best interest. Not this team and I didn't give a fuck about him building relationships for other clients, present or future.

This had just fucking happened to my brother Urban. He'd been traded and his agent hadn't gotten the chance to tell him that it was even possible. That was how he'd ended up on my mom's team in Kalamazoo. Grandpa still owned the team, but Mom ran it so it was effectively hers.

"What?" Because it still wasn't clear.

"I don't want you on my fucking team," Doug said through clenched teeth.

"You don't like winning?" Because it was undeniable that I was one of the best in the league right now. Only getting better by the day.

Doug Johnson scowled. "I like my players to have a certain character and you don't have it."

Walt sighed again. "This is about his daughter Hannah." When nothing about her registered for me, Walt rubbed his hand over his forehead. He was clearly uncomfortable with what was happening, but I didn't even understand what it was yet.

"She's pregnant," Doug said like an accusation.

I raised my hands then lowered them. "Congratulations." What else was I supposed to say?

"Don't take that tone with me." Doug Johnson seemed ready to come across the desk at me. "I don't want deadbeats on my team. You're out. You're just lucky that your mommy owns a team so you have somewhere to go. No one else would take you."

I found that hard to believe and that wasn't me being full of myself. There was no denying my game right now. My ERA was low and ticking lower by the game—I was getting better every game. Hell, when we played the National League, I could even bat, which was unusual for a pitcher since in the American League, we never batted. We used the designated hitter instead.

"Do you think I had something to do with your daughter being pregnant?" I finally asked.

"We know you did," he countered. "And when she told you, you said some awful things. I'm not going to pay some asshole to ignore my daughter and their child."

I pushed to my feet but wasn't aggressive in any way. That wasn't the way out of this. The decision was made. "I've never met your daughter."

"There are pictures of the two of you at a party."

Now I furrowed my brows in confusion. How the fuck could that be? At least, that was what I thought until it clicked. "Wait a minute. I did meet her at a party. Like a month ago."

Johnson got an all too-satisfied look on his face.

"I didn't take any pictures with her and I sure as hell didn't get her pregnant."

"She says differently."

"Well, she's a liar, then," I countered and it probably wasn't smart, but what did I have to lose? "Oh, she was definitely trying to get me to take her for a ride, but I said *no*. She said she'd wanted me for a while, which... yeah. Look at me, but no. I didn't fuck her, so she's someone else's problem."

"Get out," Johnson spat.

I shook my head. "You're going to trade me because of your daughter, who I don't even know? You don't want a paternity test to prove it or anything? Because I'm happy to take it. I know what it'll show."

His face reddened. "How dare you speak about my daughter that way? Get out. You're done. Get your shit out of the clubhouse immediately."

There was no arguing this. He'd made up his mind and there wasn't anything I could do about it. In the end, it'd be his loss. Someone else would pick me up... Wait. He'd said I was lucky my mother owned a team...

Shit.

None of us wanted to be on my mom's team. Brooks had been drafted there and stayed. Silas had gotten traded to the team two seasons ago and seemed to like it. Especially after he'd hooked up with Amity Kincaid, the woman he'd wanted since he was a teenager but had gotten too much in his own way about it. Then Urban had been traded there this year. He hated the idea. Probably still does, but he was with his girl, Everly, now and I didn't think wild horses could drag him out of Kalamazoo—at least not willingly.

I was the only one of us not on the Knights and fuck… This meant that Grandpa's dream of having all of us on the same team was going to come true.

But I'd sworn to never be on the Knights. I'd take a pay cut if I had to.

As I stormed down the hallway of the office to head back down to the clubhouse to clean out my locker, I pulled my phone out from my pocket and selected my mother's contact.

"Hey, Cobb," she answered, as if she wouldn't have known why I was calling.

"Mother." It was all I said and it was all I needed to say.

"Don't take that tone with me, Cobb," she said gently. "I didn't do this. I didn't reach out to them. *They* reached out to *me*. What was I supposed to say? *No?*"

"I have a right to refuse in my contract," I reminded her. That meant that I could refuse to be traded to any team I didn't want to go to. It didn't mean that New York would have to play me. They could release me and still pay my contract if I refused all the other teams.

"I know that," she countered. "And you can refuse. Doug Johnson can kick you off their team— you can't refuse that. Sure, they'd still have to pay you, but you wouldn't be playing and I think you'd go crazy not playing."

"There are a bunch of other teams," I said, as if she didn't know that.

"There are," she agreed. I stopped walking because I didn't want to be having this conversation with my mother in the clubhouse, where the rest of the team could come and go. "And you can get Jason to work them. But that will mean a new contract. You'd have to agree to dissolve your current one. And no one knows why Johnson booted you, so there're going to be questions and there's a bit of a black cloud hanging over you." She paused then groaned. "Well, fuck."

It wasn't too often that I heard my mother swear in general, but that word was the rarest. That couldn't mean anything good.

"Well, they *didn't* know. I just got an email saying that Johnson's daughter is threatening to do and interview about you and her pregnancy." I pulled the phone away from my ear, fighting the urge to throw it against the wall, then took a deep breath and returned it. "You really shouldn't shit where you eat." No idea what else she'd said before that.

"I didn't, Mother. She's lying. I didn't fuck her. I didn't get her pregnant. I did, however, turn her down." And Peters said that she didn't take rejection well and was vindictive.

So… had she really gotten pregnant and was blaming it on me or was she lying about all of it? Actually, I didn't care.

"Now," Mom said with a calm voice. "I will honor your current contract and salary. I don't care about the rumors and as a bonus, you'll be with your family to weather this storm." She paused like she had when we'd been kids. "But it's up to you."

I groaned. There was no real choice here. I had to play. If I stopped now, what the fuck would I do with my life? "When would I pitch next?"

"With our schedule, I talked to the manager and it'd be in six days."

"Fine," I said through gritted teeth. "I'm driving myself back, then." At least I'd get a few days to myself.

"I think that's a great idea." She cleared her throat. "I'll also set you up a meeting with our lawyers." Before I could protest, she continued. "You need to talk to them to see what can be done about this situation, Cobb. She's dragging your name and as much as you might want to just let it slide, if she's what you said she is, she'll keep ramping it up. We have to deal with it."

"Fine," I said, but this time, it wasn't as harsh. My mom was just trying to help me out and I should've been more grateful.

"All right. I'll see you in a few days. Do you want to stay at home until you find a place?"

Fuck no, but it made the most sense. "Yeah. I'll stay there, but I'm not in the mood for Dad. And I'll get Camden to help me find a place after I get there." She'd just done that for my brother and as much as my sister liked to bitch about us brothers, she loved us and would do anything for us, as we would've her.

Mom chuckled. "She's going to love this."

Then we ended the call.

Now I had six days—less than, really— to get my ass back to Kalamazoo, Michigan, where I'd grown up. Before today, returning to had seemed like the worst thing that could happen.

Now, I needed to have a word with my agent because there was no fucking way he should've let me walk into that bullshit without warning.

CHAPTER 2
MONROE

"Monroe Phillips," the deep voice called out, making me hurry to my feet. The officer was so tall that I had to crane my neck to look up at him once he'd gotten close enough.

The jail cells here in Kalamazoo didn't look like what they did on TV cop shows. It wasn't all bars. This had three walls made of concrete block and the front wall was made of something else... plexiglass, maybe. I didn't know because I never wanted to touch it.

The officer opened the door and stood back. "You've made bail."

Of course I had and I bet the person who'd

bailed me out was pissed as hell. "Thank you," I told him, as if he'd been the one to do it.

But I'd been arrested enough times to have learned that the nicer you were to the police who were arresting you, the nicer they'd be to you.

The tall, Latino officer led me out to the area where they'd give me my purse, which had, of course, been thoroughly searched, then I'd be released.

"You know, you could give your dad a break," he said as we walked.

"You know my dad?" Of course he did. Everyone at the police station knew my dad. "Then you know my dads are the reason that you've ever met me."

He chuckled. "That much is true, but you know you can do what you do within the confines of the law."

I shrugged. "Maybe, but that doesn't always get the message across."

He sighed and shook his head then went behind the desk to do whatever it was they did back there. In all the times I'd been arrested, I still didn't know how this worked on their end.

"Here ya go. Good luck."

Yeah. If he knew my dad, he'd know my dad was pissed right now and that I'd need the luck.

The door buzzed for me to walk through and after seven long hours, I was a free woman. Eh. I'd had to wait longer before. Then I saw my dad and the severe look on his face and I kind of wished I could go back into the holding cell.

After putting my purse over my shoulder cross-body style, I approached him.

Dad was dressed for work in a sharp as hell, expensive suit. His brown hair with the brushes of gray at the temples was perfectly coiffed in his normal style. The one that said he was a lawyer and wasn't messing around.

"Hello, Father," I said so much more formally than we normally spoke, but this was our normal when he picked me up from a police station. No. This wasn't the first time.

"Monroe." Then he turned and walked out of the building, fully expecting me to follow. Of course I did because he was my ride home. I hadn't had my car with me last night and even if I had, it would've been impounded or would still be in the parking lot of the bar we had left.

It wasn't until we were in his luxury, black

Jaguar with the leather seats that felt like butter that he sighed and looked over at me.

"*Again*, Monroe? Really?" He sounded more exasperated than angry. After all, he was a very high-powered criminal defense lawyer whose daughter had just gotten arrested… again.

"It was for a good cause."

"The fourth time? The fourth time is for a good cause?" He threw his hands up in the air and let them drop in frustration. "What was it this time, Monroe?"

I took a deep breath then blew it out slowly. "Maybe it wasn't a good cause."

He nodded. "I figured as much, given that I can't think of any actual good cause that would make you throw a brick through someone's car window at two in the morning." This was back to his normal dad voice. "Come on, tell me what happened. You know I can only help you if you tell me everything."

That was true and I normally told my dads everything, anyway. The other three times I'd been arrested had been during protests. They'd raised me to be socially aware and change things when I could. Though after the second arrest, they'd asked me to tone it down a bit, knowing that I wasn't going to do that at all, but this… this was different.

"It wasn't a cause. I got angry."

He closed his eyes slowly then opened them. "We've told you to use your anger in productive ways. That's how we raised you. You're well aware, Monroe, that your actions have consequences and not just for you. You're twenty-one years old, about to graduate from college. You need to—"

I cut him off. "It wasn't just that I got angry. You remember Owen, right?"

He nodded. "The temporary boyfriend whom you weren't in love with and weren't heartbroken over."

I snorted. I'd said those very words to him and Papa so many times to assure them that I didn't need to wallow. We'd dated for two very brief months when I'd realized that he'd paid a lot of attention to every pretty girl we'd come in contact with while ignoring me. That wasn't a heartbreak. He had just been kind of shitty as a potential boyfriend and I wasn't here for that.

"Right. I was out with the girls last night. We were having fun." He'd know I meant my two best friends I'd had since elementary school. Asher and Kiana and I had been inseparable since second grade. Now, we all went to different schools and since it was summer, they were both back in town. Which meant it was time to catch up and have some fun. "Owen was at that bar. I didn't care."

"Mm-hmm." That didn't sound like he believed me, but I let it go.

Not every breakup was a heartbreak.

"Anyway," I said pointedly. "He was there. When we were leaving, we were outside and he was too. But he was harassing an acquaintance of mine who was there with his boyfriend. He was harassing them about being gay. Sure, Owen was drunk, but he was saying shitty things thinking he was funny."

Dad's face softened. "What things?"

I shook my head. "I'd rather not repeat them. But what was I going to do? Fight him? I didn't think it was a good idea, so I grabbed a brick from the alley and smashed his window to get his attention off them and on me." I bit my lips together quickly. "I might have also kicked his car, which resulted in a dent."

Dad rubbed his forehead with his thumb and finger then sighed. "Monroe."

"I know. Not the smartest thing I could've ever done. He just... I saw red," I said. And Dad would know why. He'd heard the stories about what Papa had gone through when he'd first come out. They stuck with me. "There's no way I could stand by and watch that happen."

Dad reached out and wrapped a strong hand over my shoulder, giving me a squeeze. "I know, sweetheart, but you could've been hurt. I need you to think about that before you do these things. I don't know what Papa and I would do if something happened to you."

"I know. I'm sorry that I make you worry, but I couldn't stand by and let that happen."

He sighed, probably because he knew there was no way for him to change my mind about what I'd done. "I'll reach out to the prosecutor. You be ready when I call."

"I will be." Pushing myself up, I wanted to kiss him on the cheek. That usually made him melt a little, though I knew he wasn't really mad at me. He was upset that I lived in a world where I could be hurt. "I'd say I'm sorry," I told him, "but you made me this way."

He chuckled and nodded his head. "I probably did. Or at least I'm half-responsible."

Dad drove me home without any more of a lecture from him. It wouldn't have done any good anyway. I wouldn't have been able to live with myself if I'd walked away and not looked back. Worse than that, I never would've been able to look my fathers in the face again.

He pulled into the driveway and told me to get some sleep, but not too much. He was going to see if he could meet with the prosecutor today and he'd want me there for it. I promised I'd just take a cat nap.

Instead of going through my entrance in the garage that led to my apartment, I went into the main house, where I knew Papa was waiting with nervous energy that wouldn't dissipate until he saw me.

Once I'd gotten through the door, something clanged in the kitchen, so I headed that way.

Papa was two years younger than Dad. He was only slightly shorter, but his hair was a medium blond without a trace of gray. Either Papa wasn't as stressed as Dad or blond hair didn't show the gray as easily. I used to think I'd gotten my straw-berry-blonde hair—blonde that had been "kissed by a strawberry," Papa used to tell me—from him, but no. That wasn't the case since we weren't biologically linked. It had to have been the donor egg that they'd used. None of it mattered to me, though,

I didn't care if Dad was biologically related to me and Papa wasn't. They were both my dad.

"Hey, Papa," I said as I slid into a seat at the island.

He turned to me and tried to look stern, but that wasn't as natural to him as it was to Dad. "Monroe Phillips. What were you thinking? Are you hungry?"

"I'm starving, actually." Papa turned to start making me breakfast. He had everything out, as if he'd just been waiting for me to get here. That was when I realized Dad had probably sent him a text that we'd been on our way. "And I was thinking I wasn't going to let someone I know get bullied."

As he cooked, I gave him the same rundown of what had happened that I'd given Dad when he'd picked me up. It was better to get it out of the way.

"Monroe. You could've been hurt." He slid the scrambled eggs onto a plate followed by two slices of bacon and a piece of toast.

"I know. I've already gotten the lecture from Dad."

"Well, you'll get it from me too." He leaned his arms on the island across from me as I shoveled a big forkful of eggs into my mouth. "I told you about what I went through because it was part of knowing me. Not to make you feel like you have to put yourself in harm's way to defend someone else."

"Papa, I wasn't in harm's way. I'm pretty sure Owen was too drunk to find me even if he'd wanted to."

"And you?"

I shook my head. He should've known better. I had rules about drinking and he knew it. "I hadn't been drinking at all. It just really pissed me off and I had to do something to get him to leave those guys alone."

Papa nodded. "I get it. I don't like it, but I get it."

"Hey, why aren't you at work?" I asked, to which he scowled.

"You think I'm going to go off and carve tables and make chairs before I know that my daughter is OK?"

"I was fine. You knew where I was and that Dad would be the one to come get me. Plus, I was alone in the holding cell. I even slept for a while."

He groaned. "You're getting far too comfortable being in a police station."

A laugh burst from my chest. They should honestly blame themselves for that. I'd been raised to be socially conscious. Was I perfect? No. But there were closely held beliefs that I'd stand up for no matter what.

Would that get me hurt one day? Maybe. I didn't think so, but it could. Though sacrifice was part of making a change, I was always careful. And Dad had coached me early on about what to say if I encountered police and what I had to comply with versus what I didn't have to comply with.

The message was mostly to keep my mouth shut until he arrived. As my lawyer, he'd do the talking.

I took four more bites of my breakfast then hopped off the stool to take my plate to the sink.

"Thanks for the food," I told him before pushing up to kiss him on the cheek. It wasn't even much of a stretch this time since he was leaning his elbows on the counter while sipping his coffee. "I'm going to get some more sleep then take a shower."

"It should be the other way around."

I waved over my shoulder and kept walking. He was right. I should've washed the jail cell off of me before climbing into bed, but a shower would wake me up and I wanted to sleep a while longer. This just meant that I'd have to change my sheets when I woke up.

Sleep kept me longer than I'd intended, but it'd been a long night and while I hadn't lied about getting some sleep in the holding cell, it hadn't been restful. At least in my own bed, I was comfortable.

Until the constant dinging of my phone woke me up. For that to happen, I must've already been on my way to waking; otherwise, it was unlikely I'd hear my phone. There were texts from my friends asking if I was OK and from my dad asking me to be home for dinner tonight. I sent him a thumbs-up and then rolled back over in my bed. I'd call Asha an Kiana later.

Eventually, I did get my butt out of my super comfortable bed and dragged it to the shower so that I could get my bedding washed and be over to their house for dinner.

I didn't exactly live with my dads. They had their house and my place would affectionately be called 'an in-law suite.' It was basically a separate apartment from their house with its own entrance and everything. So they were right there, but I had some independence. I'd chosen a local university with a great Political Science program and could commute, but they also wanted me to be responsible for my own place without having the added pressure, I guess.

I didn't have to pay rent or the utilities. Dad and Papa agreed that I wouldn't be paying that if I'd decided to live in a dorm. They'd pay it as part of my tuition but I had to keep the place up, clean up after myself. All the things I would've had to do anywhere I lived.

The bedding was already washed, dried, and put back on my bed by the time Papa came in with pizza and Dad had joined us. Dad took the pizza to the table while Papa got the plates and I rounded up what everyone wanted to drink.

I liked to have dinner with my dads and did it often, though when school was in session, I didn't always have the time. Eventually, I'd graduate— next year—and move out, but right now, I kind of loved living close to them while also having my own space.

Thought they were clear that there was no rush for me to move even after graduation. Multi-generational houses were normal in other parts of the world and they loved me being close.

"Did you find something out?" I asked once the three of us had sat at the table in the kitchen. There was a formal dining room, but we rarely ever used it.

"I set up a meeting," Dad said. He was still wearing the same suit he'd picked me up in this morning, but now the tie was loose and the top couple of buttons were undone. He'd also lost the jacket somewhere.

"A meeting?" I asked. I'd figured he'd just deal with the whole thing because he had before.

Dad nodded while Papa watched him intently. "We're going to meet Monday morning with the prosecutor and probably Owen to see if we can work out a deal."

"A deal?" This was all new to me. In the past, I'd been booked for protesting and not leaving when I'd been told to. It was basically a ticket that was paid and I got to move on with my life. But this… this was different.

"Yes. Hopefully, Owen will agree to drop the charges if you agree to pay for the damages."

"And probably stay away from him," Papa added.

I groaned. "Staying away from him won't be an issue. I didn't mean to go around him last night. He was just here."

"Whatever the case may be," Dad continued, "you'll have to get a job to pay for the damages."

I nodded, having figured that would be the case. I'd wanted to get a summer job, anyway, but there was zero chance either of them would be all right with me dipping into my college fund to pay for this.

"You're in luck," Papa said as I took a bite of pepperoni pizza. "One of my guys' wife owns a coffee shop. He mentioned they need some summer help."

After swallowing the pizza, I smiled. "Sounds perfect."

Was it my dream to work in a coffee shop? No. But I needed the job and this meant I could start sooner.

"Listen." Dad leaned onto the table with his hands folded in front of him. He and Papa were a lot alike. Both were tall, though Papa had more muscle than Dad because Papa worked with his hands. Personality-wise was where I really meant. They were both calm, collected kind of dudes and neither ever panicked when I got into trouble.

Dad had only yelled at me, I mean really yelled at me, once and that was because he'd been afraid. I'd done something stupid, which had put me in harm's way and that had scared him. Otherwise, the two of them were big on talking things out.

"I need you to find a way not to react with violence in the future," Dad continued.

I nodded. "This was a one-time thing. I promise. It was just…"

He held his hand up. "I understand, but let's make sure it doesn't happen again."

After agreeing, they dropped the subject. Monday morning, I'd find out whether Owen was going to be reasonable or not.

My guess was not, but I wasn't sure how far he'd push this.

CHAPTER 3
COBB

*B*eing back in the bedroom I'd grown up in, knowing that it wasn't just for a visit, was weird as fuck. It was my room, but at the same time, it wasn't or it hadn't been in years. I'd gone to college—didn't finish because I entered the draft after my sophomore year the same as my brothers, though Urban and Silas might have been after their junior year. By the time we'd gotten to me, it was a given I'd be drafted. It was just a matter of where and I didn't want it to be Kalamazoo. Again, like my brothers.

Now we were all fucking here, though I didn't know if they knew I was coming. I didn't tell them and my mom could've gone either way. She was good about giving us space when she knew we needed it. I'd gotten in sometime in the middle of the night and then crashed, hoping I'd wake up after my parents had left for work or whatever my dad did during the day.

After a quick shower, I headed down to the kitchen for a little breakfast. I'd taken my time driving here from New York, even though I should've just flown. Driving meant missing two days of workouts, but I didn't think it'd matter. I'd make sure of it with my workouts the next two days.

This huge house was quiet without four boys and a girl running around like feral animals. Boy, were they going to be surprised to see me today.

Normally, I would've at least let Camden know then she could be the town crier and tell everyone, but this time, it would come with questions. Ones that I didn't want to answer. At least not right away.

I'd found out Wednesday that I was going to Kalamazoo and left the next day after quickly setting up for movers to pack the apartment up and move everything here. Today was Saturday and I had to show up for the workout to pitch Monday night. But first, I was going to my mother's office because I hadn't talked to her since I'd called her on Wednesday.

Oh, shit. Before I did that, I'd have to unload my car. Most of my things were arriving today by mover to a storage unit I rented online. Until I got my own place, I didn't need those things. I'd only brought my essentials in the car with me, but still, it had to be unpacked. We had some house staff, but I wasn't going to ask them. It only took two trips.

Then I was on my way to my mother.

Everyone greeted me as I made my way back to her office. They'd know I was her kid and never stopped any of us from going back there. We'd been doing it since birth basically given that Grandpa has been here most hours of the day at least during the season.

Mom's office door was open, but she was on the phone, so I strode in quietly and sat in the chair across from her. She'd redone this office when she'd taken over for Grandpa. Everything was light, airy, and clean. Modern.

Once she'd hung up the phone, she sat back in her chair and folded her hands in front of her. Mom's hair was blonde and cut into a professional style above her shoulders. Today she was wearing a dark-blue silk shirt and probably dress pants. She tended to prefer them.

"I knew I heard something in the house late last

night." The corner of her mouth twitched. "Thought we might have raccoons."

I snorted. "Just me."

"You got in late."

"I did that on purpose."

She sighed. "You took your time getting here."

I shrugged. "Not often I have the time to take."

That much was true. Until the off-season, most of my time was spoken for.

Mom leaned forward so that her elbows were on the top of the desk. "All right. Tell me everything."

It was the last thing I wanted to do, but she was right. I had to tell her my side completely. We'd already talked, but I hadn't given her the details. But first, I got up to shut the door. The last thing either of us needed was for someone to overhear this private conversation. Then I was back in my chair.

"I sort of met... fuck. I don't even remember her name," I admitted. Mom scowled, though she probably thought I had slept with that woman and was denying it. Then I snapped my fingers as the name came back to me. "Hannah. I met her at this party that I didn't want to be at. She suggested we be doing something else." Because talking to your mother about a woman asking you for sex was weird as fuck. "I declined. She pushed. I still said *no* and we went our separate ways. Like a month later, I'm in the GM's office and Johnson wants me out. He said his daughter is pregnant and it's mine. Doesn't want me there if I'm going to ignore his daughter and our kid."

Mom nodded as I spoke. When I was done, she said, "And you're sure you didn't have sex with her?"

I narrowed my brows. "I think I'd remember."

"Not all men do."

That was true, but… "I do."

"All right." She blew out a breath. "Why would she say it's you, then?"

I shrugged. "How the fuck would I know? I don't know her other than the thirty second exchange we had. Peters did say she's vindictive. It's probably that."

Mom slightly cocked her head to the side, which told me I was being a little aggressive with her and I didn't mean to be. Mom was the one person in our lives who always had our backs. She might not have always been around due to work, but we could go to her and she wouldn't lose her shit like Dad.

I held my hands up in surrender before dropping them back on the arms of the chair. "I don't know, Mom."

"Tell me exactly what happened."

I let out a long sigh and told her everything again, trying not to forget a single detail. Mom was the one who would help me out of this jam, so if she needed to hear it a hundred times, I'd tell her, but I didn't know what good it would do.

"OK." She sat back in her chair, that line between her eyebrows appearing. We'd seen that over and over again when we'd been kids. Whenever she was serious, disapproved, or was chastising us, that line appeared. "I'm going to get you an appointment with our lawyer right away on Monday."

"What if he doesn't have an appointment on Monday?"

Mom chuckled. "He'll make time."

She was very used to getting what she wanted in the business world and truthfully, whatever lawyer she was talking about, Mom was probably his highest-profile client, which meant I would be too.

"What if this gets out?" That was the kicker. I'd spent most of my life trying not to bring bad press to our family... Hell, we all had. We'd done shit when we'd been kids, but we'd kept our noses clean of anything like this.

Would it be a sex scandal? The rich guy turning his back on his own kid—something none of us would do? Fuck… I just wanted it to be over.

"If it gets out, we'll handle it. Just you don't say anything if anyone asks. Your brothers and sister… in private. Teammates—nothing. And of course if a reporter were to ask, you have no comment." I opened my mouth to say I wanted to defend myself, but she stopped me. "I don't care, Cobb. You say nothing or no comment. Either will work, but there's no point in defending yourself in the court of public opinion. It won't work."

She wasn't wrong. And the chances of me saying something without making it worse was actually slim to none. People liked to take a woman's side by default and usually, it was the right thing to do. I couldn't blame them. Most likely, no one would believe me.

"I'm not glad of the circumstances," she said quietly, "but I am glad that you're here. Make sure you go see your grandpa. He's like a kid on Christmas morning."

I nodded then pushed out of the seat and told her I'd see her later.

My brothers needed to know what was going on and from what Mom had said, she hadn't told them.

Though my first workout wasn't until tomorrow, I went down to the clubhouse, anyway. Mom's office was way upstairs, but I was here, and they'd see me tomorrow. Not to mention, the trade was probably going to be announced today. It seemed like everyone wanted this done quietly, but it was only a matter of time before it was on every sports channel at the very least.

There wasn't anyone in the clubhouse when I arrived. This was almost like church for me. A place for quiet and calm—at least when no one else was there. When it was full, it may as well have been the middle of Times Square with the noise, but right now… it was pretty perfect.

But I didn't have a cubby yet. They were basically lockers without doors and way bigger than we'd had in high school. There was no need for doors and locks here.

"I'm sorry. Do my eyes deceive me?" That was my brother Urban's voice.

I snorted and turned around. "I'm a mirage."

He started toward me then brought me in for a hug. "What the fuck are you doing here?"

This made me sigh. I'd have to tell them all, but I didn't have to tell them one by one. "I'll tell you once the others are here." He'd know that I meant our brothers and not the whole team. "I don't want to do this more than once."

One by one, they trickled in and we greeted each other the way I'd greeted Urban. They of course all asked the same question. Mom really hadn't told them that I was coming today. She was leaving it up to me how much I wanted to tell them, which would be all of it. These were my brothers.

"Why don't you all get cleaned up and we'll grab lunch?" I told them. "I'll explain then."

They agreed and headed off to the showers. They'd done their morning workouts but now had time before they needed to be back for the game. I hadn't decided if I was going to watch the game tonight or not. I was leaning toward not. I still had to unpack.

Once they were ready, we headed out. Brooks drove the four of us to the closest restaurant that had healthy options. I could've gone for a big burger at Cleats & Kegs, but I didn't have to play a baseball game in a few hours. We got ourselves settled and ordered before Brooks took over.

"What the hell are you doing here, Cobb? You missed your last start. What's going on?"

"I missed my last start because I'm not on that team anymore."

"What the fuck?" Silas snapped. "What happened?"

"I've been traded. Here."

All three sets of their eyebrows shot up. "What?" Urban finally asked. "I just told Mom you were never coming here. There wasn't anything she could do because that's what you told me."

I shrugged. "The universe heard that and said, 'I take that bet.'"

"What happened?" Brooks asked more seriously.

I took a deep breath then told them the story. It was becoming redundant by now, but I figured they should know what was going on because it could eventually affect them to some extent. If one of us was getting dragged in the press, the rest of us would be asked about it. That came with the whole *being brothers all playing professionally* thing.

"That's so fucked up," Silas said as soon as I'd finished.

"Especially since you're not even the best brother," Urban offered. I shoved him and caused him to laugh. He was fucking with me. We all did it.

"Yeah, I'm sure Amity and Everly would really appreciate it if this was one of you." I hadn't met Everly yet, but it was a safe assumption. Amity I knew from high school. We'd graduated together, so with her, I knew for a fact that she'd rip my brother's balls off then ask if the story was true.

"Uh…" Silas offered. "No, they would not." Our food had arrived while I told them everything that had happened and why I was here. He took a bite of his chicken then asked, "So what are you going to do?"

"Meeting with a lawyer on Monday to find out."

"You know, if you don't want to stay with Mom and Dad, you could move into the apartment where I'm living," Urban told me. "I can stay with Everly until I find the right house."

"That's probably a good idea. I haven't run into Dad since I just got home and have been wondering how long I can keep that streak going."

Silas groaned. "Not long enough, I bet."

But I didn't see him before I moved my few things into Urban's apartment, which was technically the team's apartment. It was big with a good view of the city and would do until I found something that was just mine. Camden would probably help with that, though surprisingly, she texted to tell me she knew everything and was sorry to hear, but I didn't see her before Monday.

There was something comforting about being back with my family during this. In New York, I'd been on my own and left pretty quickly. If I had stayed, I would have isolated myself out of worry that others would hear what had happened. Now, my family knew and I could go to them for support if I needed it.

And after a weekend of pitcher workout, I was at the lawyer's office Monday morning telling this fucking story again. His office was across the street from the courthouse and next to this coffee shop I knew I'd be hitting after I was done here. Technically, I needed to report to the field early, but Mom had made everyone who needed to know aware of the fact that I'd be there as soon as I could be.

Which meant there was time for coffee.

But first, dealing with this.

Manning, the lawyer, was tall and thin and wore an expensive suit. His hair was brown without any hint of gray, though he had to be my dad's age. He was behind this huge, dark-wooden desk listening to the details of the fucking story I had to tell again. He needed to know everything and stopped me several times to ask if I'd touched her when I said something or had she given me a look.

But I hadn't touched her at all. Not even innocently.

"OK," he said with a heavy sigh. "This should be easy enough. You'll have to take a paternity test. I'm sure that won't be a problem."

"Not for me," I told him. "Happy to do it. Can I do it now?"

He smiled, but it wasn't with humor. "Not today, anyway. I'll reach out to her to get her lawyer's information. That won't be hard. I'm sure they're planning on filing something. If nothing else, I'll get a hold of her dad. He's more public, so it'd be even easier."

True. As the owner of the team in New York, he had a very public profile.

"But until I can contact them, there's nothing to do. She might refuse a paternity test until the baby is born. It's hard to force that, so don't get discouraged if we can't."

"Why can't we force it?"

"They're not asking for anything at this point. Normally, we'd file for a paternity test after the other side filed for child support. She's not doing that and can't do it easily before the baby is born. The only other way would be to admit you had relations with her and want to stake your claim on the kid."

"Well, that wouldn't be true."

"Exactly. So we aren't going to do that."

"So it could be months?"

He nodded. "It could be, but I don't think it will be. I'll have a better feel for it once I find out what they want and if she'll do the test. Given the timeline you've told me, she wouldn't be able to do a test now, anyway. I think she'd have to be nine to twelve weeks along and it sounds like she'd be more like four to six. I'll double check all of that so we get it done as soon as we can."

My blood boiled. Best-case scenario, I'd have this hanging over my head for three to six weeks. And that was best-case scenario.

"What if the press gets a hold of it?" I asked because if it could remain quiet for however long it took to do the test, I could live with that.

"If that happens, we'll take care of it. They

can't accuse you of things like that." He paused then shrugged. "Well, they can, but when we prove you're not the father, we can sue them for defamation. Don't worry about this, Cobb. I'm good at what I do. I'll make things clear with her lawyer today."

After shaking his hand, I left his office feeling like this wasn't going to impede on my life for long. Optimistic, I'd almost say. Though it had already fucked things up. I was in Kalamazoo, where I didn't want to be, on a team that I never wanted to play for.

At least there was someone doing something about it.

As I'd planned, I headed over to the coffee shop for a coffee and once I was there realized I was starving, so I also grabbed a breakfast sandwich then took a seat at the long table. Since this place was across from the courthouse, it was busy as hell. All the single seats were taken and in the middle was one long table with chairs all around it. I didn't care. I just wanted to scarf down this sandwich.

Just after I'd finished it and balled the paper up, a long, frustrated sigh came from beside me.

There was a woman there. Beautiful with strawberry-blonde hair, angry, blue eyes and a tight jaw.

Though the freckles on her nose as well as her short stature made her anger seem not as scary as I thought it probably was.

"Can you move your bag?" she asked the man sitting two chairs from me and it did not sound like a request.

"Excuse me?" he asked while looking her up and then down in that gross way guys did when taking inventory of a woman's assets, which irritated me. There was a way to do it without being gross. I could only imagine how she felt about it.

"Move. Your. Bag." She didn't raise her voice, which I thought probably made it worse. "Bags don't get chairs. There's not another free one. I'd like to sit, so please move your bag."

The guy furrowed his brows and right as I was about to say something to him, he snatched the bag off the chair beside me so that she could sit down with her iced… coffee of some kind. Then he grumbled and got up from the table. I watched as he left the coffee shop just to make sure he wasn't coming back.

"Bad day?" I asked her, for what reason, I had no idea. It would've been smarter to keep my mouth shut and head to the ballpark.

"You wouldn't believe me if I told you," she said, not looking over at first.

It took everything for me to not chuckle. I'd had a shit start to my morning as well. "Try me," I told her and she finally looked over then took a deep breath.

CHAPTER 4
MONROE

*W*hat a joke.

My face was pinched together as I stared at the asshole sitting across from me and I let out a long, exaggerated sigh as my toes tapped against the tile floor. I couldn't even fully reach the damn floor. A major downside to being short was my feet swung like I was a damn kid sitting at the adults' table.

"I think if she were to pay restitution for the cost of repairing the car that she damaged, we can close this." The prosecutor didn't look excited to be sitting at this table with us.

Dad had explained that things didn't move this quickly most of the time, but since we were looking for me to not make it to court, it should be a lot quicker. Now I was spending Monday morning across from the asshole I'd barely dated, tapping my fingers against the wooden table, trying not to say anything that would get me into more trouble.

"Perfect," I said, which brought a scowl from my dad. I'd forgotten. I wasn't supposed to talk. Besides that, Dad raised an eyebrow. Yeah, yeah. I knew I had to get a summer job, but school hadn't been out long.

I'd been told in no uncertain terms that I was *not* to do any talking unless my dad said to. Sitting there quietly was incredibly difficult. I wanted to burst from my skin. Owen was acting as if he'd done nothing wrong and I was the psycho who'd attacked for no reason.

But that was bullshit.

The corners of Owen's mouth turned up in a "cat who ate the canary" sort of way and I wasn't going to like what came out of his mouth next.

"I'm not sure I'll be happy with just reparations," he said, not taking his eyes off me.

Of course he wasn't. A dull ache began between my eyes and the heat that washed over me had me wanting to burst into flames.

"Would you rather twenty-five to life?" my father asked with the most sardonic tone. "Let's be serious. Even if we went to trial, she's likely to get off with probation."

"She has a record," Owen countered, making the biggest mistake of his life. There was zero chance he'd be able to hold his own against my father.

Dad chuckled. "For protesting. She has no record of violent or destructive behavior. It will be probation." As if brushing Owen off, Dad went back to speaking only to the prosecutor.

The prosecutor narrowed his eyes at the asshole also known as Owen. "I think paying restitution is the main thing here. We can enter that in. It would be a guilty plea, but she could petition to have it expunged in a year if she keeps her nose clean."

I bit my lips together. Was it likely I'd throw another brick through a car window in the next year? No. I'd make sure my anger didn't get away from me again.

Dad nodded. "I think we can agree to that."

"I'll get the agreement drawn up and send it over."

The prosecutor reached his hand out and Dad took it then motioned for me to stand up. We were leaving the office while the prosecutor was still talking to Owen. At least I wouldn't see him in the elevator, which was where I waited for us to be before asking any questions.

"So I just have to pay what it cost to fix his car?" I asked as soon as the doors closed. We were alone in this elevator.

"Yes. But you make that sound so easy." He turned to me. "You have to pay, Monroe. That doesn't mean you get to dip into your dads' accounts to make it happen."

"I know. I'll get a job. I was going to for the summer, anyway."

The doors opened with a *ding*, so the two of us stepped out and crossed the lobby.

Dad sighed. "Your papa has a friend who owns the coffee shop right there across the street. He's always looking for extra help. I'm sure he can make a call."

Did I want to work in a coffee shop as my long-term goal? No. But it was kind of perfect for the summer.

"I'll do whatever I have to do to pay for this."

Dad nodded and his face softened. "I know you will. Most likely, we'll pay it and have you pay it back because I don't want that fucker to have anything to hold over you."

I reached out and wrapped my arms around his waist. "Thank you, Dad."

My dads had money. They weren't uber wealthy that I knew of, but Papa's furniture sold well and was incredibly pricey and Dad's law practice was insanely busy. I'd heard how much he charged per hour for his services and had almost swallowed my tongue.

"What are you going to do now?" he asked once I'd released him.

"Probably go over there and get some coffee. Owen gave me a headache and caffeine is always good for that." Though that headache was subsiding now that I was away from Owen.

"Good idea. Get the lay of the land." He glanced at his watch then back to me. "I've got to get back to the office. I have a meeting in fifteen minutes."

"Go. Have a good day."

I stood there on the street watching him as he hurried around the corner until I couldn't see him anymore then waited for traffic to clear so that I could hurry across the street.

The coffee shop was so busy, which if I worked here would be good and bad. Good because the day would go by fast. Bad because I'd be dead at the end of my shift. But what did I expect of a coffee shop across the street from the courthouse where everyone who went in or out was stressed to the max and likely need a jolt to stay awake or calm down?

But I was patient now. Without the asshat around, I could wait for my iced coffee all day if I needed to. OK. That might've been an overstatement. Still, I was patiently waiting, trying to let the meeting that morning slide off my back so that Owen didn't take up any more of my time.

Once I had the coffee in hand, I planned to have a seat for a few minutes and mindlessly scroll my phone. Except there weren't any seats. At first, I figured I'd take my coffee and go, but I had really just wanted to sit, enjoy the good stuff, while scrolling on my phone. Not to mention Owen would be leaving the courthouse, if he hadn't already, and the last thing I wanted was to run into that asshat on the street.

That was when I noticed a free chair at the long table in the middle and hurried over to it. But the jerk in the seat next to it had his bag on it. At first, I didn't know whose it was until the guy to my right reached into it for something.

"Can you move your bag?" I asked the man

who'd just reached into the bag. Sure, I worded it as a question, but didn't actually mean it as a request. I just wanted to sit down and scroll on my damn phone, but this guy was either a jerk for taking up a second seat in a very busy coffee shop or he was oblivious to what was happening around him. Either way, I wanted him to move the bag.

"Excuse me?" he asked while looking me up and then down at the bag slowly, which made me want to kick him in the shins. Another asshole wasn't what I needed right now.

This guy was good-looking enough but was far too put-together for my taste. Perfectly styled blond hair and sparkling, brown eyes made me wonder if he had eye drops to create the sparkle. Even if I hadn't been in the mood I was currently in, I wouldn't have liked this. He looked at me as if his answer to my question was based on my looks.

"Move. Your. Bag." I didn't raise my voice. Honestly, I almost never raised my voice in anger unless the room around me was loud. Quiet rage seemed to work the best for me. "Bags don't get chairs. There's not another free one. I'd like to sit, so please move your bag."

The guy furrowed his brows but didn't move, which made me glance around again just to make sure something else hadn't opened up for me. It wasn't like I wanted to sit next to this guy, anyway. Then suddenly, he snatched the bag off the chair so I could sit down then mumbled under his breath and hopped up from the table. He hurried out the door like his ass was on fire.

I shrugged and took the open seat then pulled my phone out of my crossbody purse.

"Bad day?" the man on the other side of me asked.

"You wouldn't believe me if I told you," I said without looking over at him. I hadn't gotten a good look at him because my focus had been on the bag in the chair and Mr. Perfect being hesitant to move it.

The deep voice said, "Try me."

I sighed again and looked up at him, fully intent on telling him to leave me alone so I could wallow in my shitty mood.

But what I found was a dark-haired, strong-armed man with a strong jaw. He was... chiseled by the great artists. He was tall... He looked tall sitting in the chair, with thick, dark hair—maybe not black, but so dark, I couldn't tell—and cocoa-colored eyes. He was... absolutely beautiful and I forgot what I'd been about to say to him.

"You all right?" he asked when I was staring for far too long.

My heart raced and my palms dampened like they hadn't since I'd been a freshman in high school and the guy I'd had a crush on had spoken to me.

"What?" I asked because whatever he'd said had gone straight out of my brain.

"I asked if you're all right."

Right. Was I? Yes. I was fine, but for some reason, with this man, who looked to be close to my age, beside me, I was a bumbling idiot.

I supposed, no. I wasn't fine, but I couldn't tell him that part of it.

"Yeah," I finally got out. "I'm fine. I just don't see why someone would take up a seat in a crowded shop for a bag. Like, have some consideration."

He chuckled quietly and the way he looked right at me was almost too much. Like I was staring into the sun. "You said I wouldn't believe your bad day?" he reminded me.

I shrugged and threw my hands in the air before letting them smack lightly onto the table. "I barely believe it."

"Try me," he said again.

For some reason, I took a deep breath and

decided to spew it all out there for this stupidly hot stranger in the coffee shop.

"I just came from the courthouse, where I had to sit through a meeting with the prosecutor and my ex-dickhead. The prosecutor just wants me to pay reparations, but the ex-dickhead isn't happy with that. *Oh, no.* I can't just pay to repair what I damaged. He won't be happy until he sees me doing fifty years in a maximum security prison. But to pay the reparation, I have to get a summer job, so I'll probably be working in this very coffee house all summer, which is fine. I like it here, but fuck, I'm over this bullshit already."

I took in and let out a deep, cleansing breath.

Unloading all of that felt good. For some reason, talking to this stranger had lifted a weight off my shoulders. Maybe I was taller now. I felt taller. Also, this man I didn't know was really easy to talk to.

"Wow," was all he said in response to everything I'd just told him. I'd figured that a lot of people would be taken aback by the fact that I'd been arrested and all that. "Is this the first time you've been arrested?"

A laugh popped out of my mouth before I could help it. Of all the things he could've asked, this was what he'd gone with. "No," I told him honestly. "But in fairness, the other times were at protests and I don't regret them."

He turned his coffee slowly with the fingers of one large hand. "So those were for good reason."

I shrugged. "I thought so."

"What'd you do this time?"

I sighed. In reality, all things considered, what I had done wasn't so bad. I mean, it wasn't good. I *had* damaged someone else's property, but I hadn't gone on a killing spree or even physically assaulted Owen, which was what I'd really wanted to do.

"Threw a brick through my ex-dickhead's car window."

His eyebrows raised and he bit into his bottom lip, as if he were keeping from laughing. "Seriously?"

I nodded. "I know it was a bad idea and honestly, I didn't think it through. Of course he'd jump at the chance to have me arrested for it."

"No. I meant *seriously, he called the cops for that?* Not seriously, you did that."

"What do you mean?"

"I mean, most guys I know would've just replaced the window and moved on. Most wouldn't call the cops unless the woman got really psycho. Did you get really psycho?"

"I don't think so." Then I realized that I probably wouldn't know if I had. That night, anger had gotten the better of me, so did that mean I didn't remember it all? "How about I tell you exactly what happened and you tell me if I went psycho?"

"Deal."

He sat up in his chair and leaned closer so I wouldn't have to talk louder. I wanted that to be on purpose. Like he was concerned for me and what everyone else might hear. Though having him closer sent a tingle up my spine and made other things happen inside my body that I didn't want to talk about.

"First," he said quieter than he had been. Some of the crowd had left the coffee shop, like they'd all been here on break or before a court time, so there was no reason to try to be heard over the noise. "Ex-boyfriend or ex-husband? And did you recently break up?"

I scoffed. "Boyfriend and no. It was months ago and we'd barely dated. I don't know that I'd call it a breakup, either. More like we just didn't go out anymore because I said *no*."

"Then why do you call him 'the ex-dickhead'?"

I shrugged. "What else should I call him? *Guy I dated for a few months* is too many words in the moment."

He chuckled deep in his chest, which made me want to see him really laugh. Like a full, belly laugh. Alas, I never would, given that we were basically two ships passing in the night... or rather two people who needed a jolt in the middle of the day in a coffee shop.

"OK," he said. "Tell me."

"We were out the other night—"

"This just happened?" I nodded. "Doesn't court usually take longer than that? I mean, to get to it if you just were arrested the other night?" He held his hands up and said, "I wouldn't know. I've never been arrested."

I snorted. "I don't know what *usually* happens. When I've been arrested before it was for protesting, like I said. They usually drop those charges unless you've done damage. I only disturbed the peace."

"So this time's different because you did damage?"

"You know what? I don't know. I could ask my dad."

"He's been arrested a lot?"

My eyes widened. If only he knew how ridicu-lous that question was when it came to my dad. "No! He's a defense lawyer, though, so he's familiar with the process."

He chuckled and I realized I didn't know his name and was now in a debate with myself as to whether I should ask it or not. It might be easier to never know. "You were saying?"

"Right." He snapped me completely out of the debate. "I was out with friends—not drinking myself because that seems to be an important point to this entire story—and we came across the ex-dickhead harassing a couple of friends of mine."

"You got mad?"

I nodded. "He pissed me off and he's way bigger than me, so it wasn't like I could physically step in, so I grabbed a brick from the alley and threw it through his car window. The harassment stopped. The friends could get out of there to avoid his wrath."

His eyes narrowed. "But you couldn't avoid it."

"He didn't do anything but yell and tower over me like he was trying to be intimidating, but since I don't intimidate—or at least not easily—it didn't work. Then he called the police."

He sighed and ran his hand over his face. "What was he harassing your friends about?"

"Being gay. It was a friend out on a date with a new guy he'd just met."

The man groaned. "That's so fucked up." The tension in my shoulders released at his response. "Seriously? It's so fucked up that homophobes are still out there."

"It is and I'm particularly sensitive to the subject and I just… saw red, I guess."

"'Particularly sensitive'?"

"I have two dads." It was the best way to explain my entire situation and my feelings on the subject. "They grew up in a different time and faced a lot of bigotry. I'm not going to stand by and watch someone else go through it and not do something."

He sighed again. "I get that. The ex-dickhead deserves a lot more than a brick through a window, but he could've hurt you. You said it was at night and you were with other friends—women, I assume from your story." I nodded. "You could've been hurt or worse. He doesn't sound all that reasonable."

"He isn't."

"So was it worth it?" he asked. I furrowed my

brows because I wasn't sure which part he meant. "Getting arrested."

"Absolutely," I told him immediately. "Dad and Papa aren't all that happy about it, but I wouldn't change a thing."

He nodded. "Then working here for the summer will be worth it too."

This man was right. If the crime had been worth it, then the penalty would be too.

Talking to this stranger gave me a whole new outlook on my situation. I'd never regretted it, but I'd been pissed when I'd left the courthouse and now I wasn't.

My only regret now was that this man was going to leave the coffee shop and I'd probably never see him again.

CHAPTER 5
COBB

*J*esus Christ, I'd never met a woman like the one sitting across from me at the coffee shop.

Too bad I was off women for the foreseeable future.

First, I hadn't even done anything and I was embroiled in a baby daddy situation in New York that hadn't hit the papers yet but could. That was one thing I was sure of. Second, the moment she found out about my situation, she'd probably run like a rat fleeing a ship because who the fuck wanted to deal with all of that, not to mention the fact that most women wouldn't want to be with someone who was shirking his responsibilities when it came to his kid.

Which I wasn't, but would she believe that?

No. It was better to keep my distance, but this woman, with her blue eyes and the freckles dotting her face looking innocent and like she could fuck up my world all at the same time had me wishing I could make a move.

Though that was likely to bite me in the ass, too.

She ran her tongue over her bottom lip quickly then took a deep breath and turned to look out the window.

"When did it start raining?" she asked.

"I don't know." I'd been too focused on her and the protective brick sitting in my stomach from when she told me she'd been basically without backup when she'd confronted the ex-dickhead who could've hurt her. Now, all of a sudden, I wanted to make sure he never could but had no idea why this feeling was raging through me.

Sure, I wouldn't want *any* woman hurt. If I saw someone trying to hurt a woman, I'd step in because it was the right thing to do and if it was my sister, I'd want someone to help her. But this was something more… and I couldn't explain it.

The rain picked up. *Fuck.* Was this going to fuck up the game tonight? If it ended soon, they could get the field ready. This was my first start with Kalamazoo and I sure as hell didn't want a rainout. I'd be bumped and it'd be five more days before I pitched. That was too long. I hadn't gone that long without pitching in a game in years.

"It's really coming down." She turned those blue eyes back on me. "I guess I should probably go."

Without breaking eye contact, I nodded slowly and said, "Yeah. Me too." I did need to get to the park to start warming up.

We both dumped our coffee cups in the trash on our way out the door. Then we stood under the overhang as a crack of thunder hit so loudly, it vibrated the ground.

"Where's your car?" I asked.

"I rode to the courthouse with my dad. I was going to take the Metro then walk." She looked out at the rain. "I probably will order a rideshare now."

"In this rain, they'll be busy. It'll take a while."

"Or I'll just wait for it to let up."

Without thinking about it too hard, I said, "I can give you a ride home."

Her lips parted, but no words came out at first. "I can't do that," she finally said. "I don't know you.

You're a guy in a coffee shop. I'm pretty sure my dads would kill me for that one."

Oh, shit. That was right. We'd never even introduced ourselves. "Sorry. I'm Cobb Briggs. And remember *I'm* not the dangerous one who just got arrested."

She snickered and the way her nose scrunched up was so fucking cute that I almost couldn't stand it. "That's true. It's across town, though. I'm sure out of your way."

"I've got time."

She nibbled on that bottom lip then nodded. "I'll take it. I really don't want to walk in the rain."

"I'm over here." I pointed around the corner where I'd parked my car, knowing that I wanted to hit the coffee shop after my meeting. Thankfully, she didn't ask why I'd been near the courthouse. It was the coffee shop across the street. Anyone could be there for reasons having nothing to do with the law.

I hit the button on my key fob so that the doors would be unlocked before we got there as we both ran through the rain. I was wearing jeans and a black T-shirt, but she was wearing a white top that women called 'a blouse,' though I didn't understand the difference between that and any other shirt that they wore, and skirt that brushed against her thighs with a pair of sandals. It was warm in Kalamazoo this time of year, but it was dressy enough to meet with a prosecutor. It had just been a meeting, after all, not court.

We each hopped in opposite sides of my car, dripping with water. I started it up and turned the heat on for a moment to help dry us off, but she was laughing.

"That was actually fun." She sat back in the seat like she didn't care that she was getting the entire thing wet. I didn't care, so she shouldn't, either, but I loved that she was comfortable.

"Getting soaked?"

She smiled widely and nodded. "Yes. It's like when you're a kid and playing in the rain. As adults, we mostly avoid it, right?" She wasn't wrong. "I'm going to go outside in the rain more," she said, like the decision was made.

"Let me know when. I'll come with you." The words came out of my mouth before I thought about how that would sound. But we could be friends, right?

Was I attracted to her? Yeah, absolutely. Too attracted to her. That didn't mean we couldn't be friends. She was easy to talk to and far more carefree than I was. All I knew was I couldn't have her in a romantic way, but not having her in my life at all was unacceptable. And no, I didn't give a fuck that I'd met her, like, an hour ago.

We were sitting in the car. Goosebumps covered her skin, so I turned the heat up a little more and reached into my back seat to grab the hoodie I knew was back there.

"Here," I said as I handed it to her. "You can dry off with it or put it on." And for the first time, I glanced down at her wet clothing and noticed that the white was slightly see-through. That was when I became a fourteen-year-old boy seeing a bra for the first time. Or at least my thoughts did because the idea of peeling that blouse off her was right there at the front of my mind.

She held up the hoodie and looked at it. It was gray and large. Probably would engulf her if she put it on, but it would work for her to get into her house. She was a lot smaller than me. Probably would come up to my shoulder at most if we were standing together and she had curves that at any other point in my life, I would've loved to get to know.

"Wait. Cobb Briggs…" She glanced at the hoodie. "Are you a baseball player?"

"Yeah."

"But don't you play for…" She got a far-off look, like she was searching her memory for the right answer. "Boston?"

I shook my head. "I played in New York. I just got traded here."

Her eyebrows shot up. "The Knights?" I nodded. "My dads are probably happy about that. They love baseball."

"And you?"

She bit her lips together briefly before saying, "I tolerate it."

I laughed loudly in the confines of my car. Normally, people tried to gush even if they didn't love the game.

"Is that bad?" she asked.

"Not liking baseball?" I asked. She nodded quickly. "I think it's a mistake because the game is the best, but you're allowed to not like baseball."

"It's not that I don't like it. I just never got into it. My dads both love it. They go to games a lot. I think Dad has season tickets. I've gone to some when Papa couldn't go, but… I'm not sure I ever figured out the rules."

"Well, I can help with that. I know them pretty well."

"Why did you get traded? Did you want to come here?" she asked. It was a question anyone would ask, but I'd just been thinking that I was glad she didn't want to know why I'd been near the courthouse.

"There are lots of reasons a player is traded and no. It wasn't my choice," I said. Her eyes narrowed, but I'd leave it at that. "For me to drive you home, I need to know where you live."

"You're not going to tell me why you got traded, are you?" She watched me with those blue fucking eyes that made me feel like she was searching into my soul, but I kept my mouth shut. She snapped her fingers. "You're right. You need my address." Then she told me so that I could get us on the road.

Before putting her seatbelt on, she yanked my sweatshirt over her and it was all I could do to not get hard.

As I drove, I told her, "You know, you never told me your name. I'm going to have start calling you 'Lawbreaker.'"

She groaned and closed her eyes as I snickered. "Please don't. My name is Monroe Phillips."

"Monroe?" I asked. It wasn't the most unusual name I'd ever heard, but it sure as hell wasn't common. Not that I had room to talk.

"That's what you get when you have two dads who love Marilyn Monroe—the feminist gay icon."

"It's a good name," I told her. "But I think I like Lawbreaker better."

She rolled her eyes exaggeratedly.

Now, I hadn't been back in Michigan long, but even in my life in New York, I wasn't sure I'd ever found someone so easy to talk to. Because we couldn't be anything else, I wanted this woman in my life as my friend.

For twenty minutes I drove with her asking me questions about baseball. Not about the game but about what I loved about the game, what I loved about playing the game, before switching to books I've read. Honestly, I didn't read a ton because I barely had time for life but the ones I had read recently she had too.

As I turned onto her street and she said, "It's three houses down."

When I pulled to a stop there, I looked over at her house. It was big. Not as big as Mom and Dad's, but I thought theirs was the biggest in the city and actually, it was technically just outside the city but close enough to still be considered part of it.

This was nice, and I'd bet more homey than ours had been growing up. It was hard to make such a large area feel homey, I supposed, though my mother did the best she could to make it that way.

"I live with my dads," she explained. "I mean… not *with* them. I have an apartment on the other side of the garage, but it's still their house. I'm in college." The words tumbled out of her mouth as if she thought I was judging her.

"It's nice to have your own space," I told her. "But it also wouldn't be a big deal if you lived in the house with them."

"I plan to move after I graduate."

"I'd probably stay if I were you."

She narrowed her eyes on me. "Do you live with your parents?"

Again, my loud laugh filled the car. "No. I haven't lived with them in a long time and not every family situation is the same."

Her face filled with questions as her lips parted again. Then she closed them. "Thanks for the ride home. And…" She tucked a piece of strawberry-blonde hair behind her ear. "Telling you all of that actually made me feel better. I don't know why. Can't explain it, but it helped."

I rested my forearm across the steering wheel as I turned toward her. "Talking to you helped too. I wasn't having the best day. Now I think it'll be all right."

She grinned right at me. "You're welcome, then." When she reached her hand out to me, I waited for her to say something. "Can I have your phone?"

I gave it to her immediately. There was no reason not to. Then she held it up to my face to unlock it and typed away. "There," she said as she handed it back. "I put my number in. In case you need another pick-me-up."

That wasn't a bad idea. Right away, I called her phone from mine then hung up once it had rung in the car. "Now you have mine in case you need to unleash your thoughts on a stranger. Or if you get into a sticky spot again. Call me instead of putting a brick through a window."

She cringed back. "That was a one-time thing. Also, are we actually strangers now? I assumed we became friends today."

One corner of my mouth turned up in a small grin. She had me there. Though I fucking hated the word 'friend' coming out of her mouth, it was all I could offer right now and it seemed it was all she wanted since she'd said it. "I guess we are. Friends, I mean. Regardless, call."

"Will do." She opened the door. The rain had lightened up, but it was still falling. "Thanks for the ride, Cobb."

"You're welcome."

Then she shut the door. She got halfway up the driveway when she kicked her sandals off and hurried into the grass. Then she threw her hands out to the sides and spun around in the rain. That was when I realized she was still wearing my sweatshirt. I didn't want it back, but it did give me an excuse to call or text her later.

Monroe spun slowly around three more times, her skirt only flying partway up, given how wet it was before her body shook with laughter and she ran over, grabbed her sandals off the driveway and headed up. Though she stomped her foot in a large puddle along the way, causing the water to splash her legs.

I watched until I couldn't see any longer admiring how carefree she was in those moments. Something she decided right here in my car. She decided then made it happen.

Now I had to get to the field.

The rain let up about an hour later while I was doing my workout. That meant the field would be fine for tonight and I'd pitch my first game with the Kalamazoo Knights.

"Why were you wet when you got here?" my brother Silas asked when we were heading back to the clubhouse from the workout room. There was time to eat, shower, dress. Then it was batting practice, which I participated in, but not on the days that I pitched.

"Got caught in the rain." Which was the truth. They didn't need any more information than that. Given that Brooks and Urban were right there with us.

"Was it a *piña colada in the pouring rain* situation?"

I stopped and looked at him. "I don't even know what that means." Then I started walking again. "I was near the courthouse this morning to meet with Mom's lawyer. Went next door for a coffee. It rained. It's not an exciting story."

"You could've lied," Urban said as he gave me a shove. "Made it interesting at least."

"What'd the lawyer say?" Brooks asked before I could respond to Urban.

"Not a lot. He's going to see what he can do about getting a paternity test in a few weeks." I shrugged then pushed through the door of the clubhouse. "I just have to wait it out and hope it doesn't hit the papers."

There wasn't anything else to say about that. We went onto the business of getting ready for the game.

I was walking out to the field to watch batting practice when my phone vibrated in my pocket. When it came time for the game, I wouldn't have it on me, but I wasn't doing batting practice today. In a short while, I'd be in the bullpen doing my own warmup.

As I continued to walk, I pulled my phone out of my pocket, saw a text from Monroe, and couldn't keep from smiling.

I forgot to leave your sweatshirt.

Now I chuckled. I'd known she'd still had it on but hadn't wanted to ask for it back. *I know*, I sent her, then followed it with, *Keep it.* Because I absolutely didn't want it back now. I wanted her to wear it.

I can give it back. I'll wash it first, though.

I shook my head and sighed. *No. Keep it.*

Then I was about to put the phone away when another text came through.

Thanks. It's really comfortable. I'll be watching the game with my dads tonight. I saw online that it said you're start-

ing. I think that means you're a pitcher, right? Anyway. Have a good game.

There was no way I'd be able to wipe this stupid grin off my face. Had she really not known I was a pitcher before? She knew I was a player, but now that she was going to be watching the game, I wanted a win even more. *Fuck.* I wanted a complete game just so I'd be the only one she was watching the entire time.

We'd have to see on that, but one thing was for certain.

I'd have to figure out a way to see Monroe again before too long. But I had to do it in a way that was friendly and didn't come off as a date. Because as much as I wanted to date that woman, I couldn't bring her into my shit and she'd made it clear that friends was the only thing on the table.

Honestly, it was probably best for both of us, though the need to know why not dating was best for her was now at the top of my list.

No matter what she was to me, I wouldn't be able to get her out of my mind.

The question was: Would she run when she found out why I was really back in Michigan?

CHAPTER 6
MONROE

"*L*eave it to Monroe to meet a sexy baseball player after being in court for fucking up someone's car," Asher, one of my two best friends, said on the video call. She had her black hair up in a bun the way she did most days when we were at school.

I rolled my eyes, but Reana giggled. "That's true. She does meet men in the weirdest places."

"One time," I said, trying to give them both the evil eye at the same time through the phone screen, while suddenly regretting calling the two of them in the first place. What was a girl to do?

I *had* met an incredibly hot baseball player in the exact manner she'd described, but it wasn't like I'd intended it to happen.

The three of us couldn't be more different. Asher was always tan with the black hair thanks to her Navajo father while Reana took after her Nordic mother. Then I fell somewhere in between with my strawberry-blonde hair and blue eyes with a smattering of freckles. I didn't know who, I looked like, if anyone, since I never saw or met the woman my dads used as a surrogate.

"So…" Reana drew out. "Are you seeing him again?"

"It wasn't like that," I told them. "He was just there and easy to talk to."

"You gave him your number, right?" Asher asked.

Well, they had me there. "Yes. Only because he said that I was the pick-me-up he needed this morning and I wanted him to have it in case he needed another."

The two of them broke out into a fit of laughter.

Once Asher had calmed down, she said, "Of course that's the reason."

"No, really," I countered. "I'm being serious. It wasn't like that." When they laughed again, I rolled my eyes and said, "I hate you both."

"No, you don't." Asher still had laughter in her

voice as she spoke. Of course I didn't hate them and if this had been one of them in my position, I would've been doing the same thing.

"Fine." I sighed. "I don't. Now, when are we getting together again?"

Reana gave me a devilish grin. "I thought we could go to a baseball game." Asher cackled as I rolled my eyes. "I mean, I'm googling that man and all I can say is… wow."

"I looked him up, too," Asher agreed. "I think they'll make really cute babies."

"What's that?" I asked, pretending like someone else had called my name. "I have to go now? Oh, no…" The deadpan tone of my voice only made them roar.

"You do not have to go."

"Actually, I do. I'm having dinner with the dads tonight. Dad insisted when he left me for the office this morning."

After Cobb dropped me off at home this morning, I'd taken a shower because I'd been soaked through and gotten dressed again. I also texted him about his sweatshirt that I'd kept and put it through the wash. All before talking to them, but I still had things I wanted to get done before I went to dinner.

Asher let out a long sigh. "Fine. Go if you must,

but we need to make plans. This is our last summer of some freedom before we have to be adults."

She wasn't wrong, but I hadn't told them that I probably had to work most of this summer to pay back damage to Owen's car. Though I couldn't imagine a window was that expensive.

We all said our goodbyes and I ended the call so that I could finish up a few more things.

Cobb's sweatshirt sat on the bed, reminding me of how it had smelled before I'd washed it. Like him and while he'd said I could keep it, I almost wished that I hadn't washed it.

Around six-thirty, I headed to my dads' house. When I opened the door, I was greeted with the most amazing aroma that I could've imagined. Something with garlic and tomatoes which was the tell-tale sign that Papa had made lasagna for dinner, which caused me to do a little excited dance. He didn't make it often because he said it took too long and most days, he didn't have the time.

But he'd done it today.

The reason it took too long was because he made everything from scratch. Except maybe the cheese, but he did have to grate it all. The pasta would be fresh and the sauce his own secret recipe.

"It smells amazing in here," I told him as I

came around the corner. He would've heard the door and known I was coming.

"Thank you."

"Did you go easy on yourself and buy the noodles at the store?"

He scowled at me. Papa came from a long line of Italian women who would've chopped his hands off if he'd used store-bought pasta. My grandma on that side had passed away last year, but her main goal in life had been to feed everyone until their stomachs burst.

"I know, I know." I held my hands up. "Grandma would come back to haunt you."

"She would and you do know it." He was working on the salad right then by chopping up a head of lettuce.

"At least you'd get to see her again."

He snorted.

"What's the occasion?" I asked.

"What do you mean?" He took the colander of lettuce over to the sink to wash it.

"The special occasion. You don't normally go through all this trouble on a random Monday. In fact…" I snapped my fingers as this occurred to me. "I'm shocked that you're home in enough time to do it on a Monday. What gives?"

He turned to me and put his hands on his hips. "Can't a man make a nice dinner for his family?"

"Of course he can. I thoroughly appreciate it." Especially knowing that I'd be taking leftovers to put in my fridge for tomorrow.

"I just thought that since we were having dinner together, anyway, that this would be nice. Your dad works hard and you both have dealt with a bunch of stress lately."

"That's all true," I agreed. "But how can you be here? You're usually in the shop until eight or later."

He shook his head as he went back to work on the lettuce. "I finished the dining table this morning. I don't handle shipping and won't be starting the next project until tomorrow."

"So half day."

"Exactly."

Papa's furniture was popular, but since he refused to mass produce anything, there was a wait-list. He had people who worked for him and once trained and to his standards, they helped, but there were projects that Papa was special requested on. Some only wanted him and they were willing to wait—and pay for—him.

The garage door came to life in the distance,

which meant Dad was home. Moments later, he came in the same door that I had.

"Lasagna?" he asked as soon as he'd turned the corner, causing Papa and me to both laugh. "What?"

"We just had this conversation," I explained. Dad nodded, then gave me a quick hug then kissed me on the side of the head before going over and kissing Papa.

"Anything I can do?" he asked.

Papa shook his head. "Monroe offered to set the table, so we're all good here."

"I did?" I asked with a grin because of course I'd set the table.

"You did."

"OK." Dad slapped his hands together. "Then I'll run upstairs to change real quick before we eat."

He hurried off while I got everything I needed to set the table.

We had a formal dining room that we almost never used when it was just the three of us. There was no sense in using that huge table, so we'd sit in the kitchen at eat at the more normal-sized one. Still big enough to bring the food to the table and it was where we'd spent most dinners when I'd been growing up.

Then we all sat down and began to dish the food out onto our plates.

"How did the rest of your day go, Monroe?" Dad asked as he added salad to his plate next to the large piece of lasagna he'd taken.

"Good."

"What'd you do?" he asked before looking over at Papa. "I think we came to an agreement today. She has to pay for the repairs to Owen's car and the prosecutor won't press charges."

"Good."

Then their eyes were back on me. "Oh, I went for a coffee, like I told you."

His eyebrows raised. "And? You couldn't have spent the entire day on a single cup of coffee."

"No." I blew out a breath. "I met someone at the coffee shop. We talked. It was good. Kind of cathartic, actually. Anyway… then I came home, showered because I'd gotten caught in the rain, talked to Asher and Reana, now dinner. That pretty much covers it."

"You had to walk from the bus in the rain?" Papa asked. "I told you she should've taken her car."

"No. It was fine. I didn't walk in the rain. The

guy I met gave me a ride home, but it was pouring and we had to run for his car."

"'Guy'?" Dad's voice told me everything I needed to know. He was suspicious. "You gave him your address."

"I mean… Yes." Then I took a bite of lasagna. "I had to for him to drop me off."

"Monroe." He sat back and sighed. "Aren't you still dealing with the last guy you dated? How many times have I told you not to trust men to have your best interest at heart?"

My cheeks heated. He had told me that my entire life. Not that all men were bad, but that I had to be suspicious until I found out if this one was a good one. Guys would say anything they thought they needed to if it meant me sleeping with them.

One benefit of two dads was that I got the straight talk about what men were like. Gay or straight, men were men.

"I know that," I told him. "That's not what this was. I…" I blew out a breath. "It wasn't the best morning, I needed coffee, this other guy… It doesn't matter. I ended up talking to this man and it felt good to unload my Owen shit on someone who didn't have an opinion." I shrugged. "I said I was taking the bus, but he didn't want me to walk in the rain. Besides, you know who he is."

Papa's eyebrows furrowed. "We know him?"

I shook my head. "You don't *know* him, but you know who he is."

"Well?" Dad asked. "Who is it?"

"Cobb Briggs. He's—"

"A pitcher for the Knights," Dad finished because of course he would. "He was just traded here. Today is his first start."

"Whatever that means," I muttered. "He was perfectly nice. Didn't do anything weird. That's all."

"Cobb Briggs was at the coffeehouse?" Papa asked. "How random."

"Yeah. I don't know why he was there." Because he hadn't told me. "But he was there."

Dad snorted. "Does that mean you're watching the game with us tonight?"

I bit my lips together and felt the heat creep up my neck.

Watching the games with them was something I did sometimes. Not all the time, but now that they knew I'd met Cobb… it might've made watching tonight weird.

But yeah. I was watching. I'd decided that earlier.

Which was exactly what I did and Cobb on the mound made it hard for me to keep the promise to myself that I'd be only friends with him—assuming he wanted that much. Dad was right. I was still dealing with the last guy I'd dated.

After the game, I got a text from Cobb asking if I'd liked the game. They'd won and it had been an exciting one, mostly because Cobb hadn't been giving up many hits, so when someone had gotten one, it had been exciting to watch to see if the other players would get the runner out.

Plus, I picked up a few more things from my dads, mostly because I was paying closer attention.

I did, but I do always enjoy it when I watch with my dads. I'm not sure if it's the game or how worked up they get.

Lol, I bet, he sent back. *Are they coming to a game anytime soon? You coming with them?*

Good question, I told him. *Dad has season tickets but doesn't go to every game. He gives away some of the tickets.*

The three little buttons popped up right away. *It's a lot of games to go to.*

Though I didn't want to stop talking to him, I also didn't know what to say, so I decided to talk to him the way I would talk to any of my friends.

I have to go back to the courthouse on Wednesday

morning to finalize the agreement. Will definitely need more coffee. Then I added an eyeroll emoji.

I bet you will, Lawbreaker.

I shook my head but couldn't keep the grin at bay. That was all he said and where the conversation ended.

Two days later, I was back at the courthouse sitting across from the prosecutor and Owen. Again. Dad said Owen didn't need to be there but had figured he would be just to fuck with me. His words.

Dad dressed like the high-priced lawyer that he was, but sometimes, his mouth sounded like a sailor's. Somehow, Papa—who looked like he'd have the potty mouth—swore way less than Dad did.

"So we're in agreement?" Dad asked the prosecutor, but he was looking directly at Owen.

"We do," the prosecutor told him. "I've explained that given Monroe's history, I have no interest in prosecuting this. There's no reason to. Not to mention the details of the event. He's satisfied with reimbursement of damages." Then he slid a sheet of paper across the table toward Dad.

"These repairs have already been done?" he asked, to which the prosecutor said they had been.

I peeked over Dad's shoulder and my stomach dropped. That total couldn't be for only a window.

After scanning the sheet, I saw that it wasn't. It was also to replace the leather on the seat as well as a couple of other things I didn't really understand.

"The leather?" I asked. "Really?"

Owen smirked. "The glass tore it."

"No, it didn't." Now this pissed me off and my heart started beating quicker and my body tensed. "There's no way—"

"This is fine," Dad said, cutting me off while angrily looking down at me. "I'll write a check right now so we can complete all of this."

"Oh so Daddy's bailing you out," Owen muttered but we all heard it. He would've wanted me to hear it.

I opened my mouth but Dad shut it with a single look. All I could do was sit there and steam.

Dad pulled his checkbook out, scribbled the amount and handed it over. Both Owen and I signed a document stating that the matter has been concluded to both of our satisfaction and Dad got something from the prosecutor that he didn't intend to press charges.

That was it. My dealings here were done and if I was lucky, I'd never see Owen again.

He left first and Dad said I had to wait the allotted time before I could leave.

"That's it?" I asked for confirmation.

"That's it as long as you don't do this again."

"I won't."

"What are you going to now?"

"Coffee." I grinned up at him.

"Of course. You drove yourself this morning, so I'm sure you'll find your way home." Dad pushed to his feet and I followed. "I'll talk to your papa tonight about reaching out to his friend at the coffee shop."

"Sounds good." Because there was no way to avoid that job and at this point, I didn't want to. I wanted to pay them back every penny.

He gave me a hug then escorted me down the elevator until we parted on the street. Dad went his way and I crossed at the corner to go to my now-favorite coffee shop.

Once I was inside, I hurried over to order my iced mocha. Right as I'd grabbed it, I noticed Cobb at an actual table by the window looking down at his phone.

Trying to hide the smile that immediately appeared when I saw him, I hurried over, hoping he wouldn't see me before I dropped into the seat across him.

"Fancy meeting you here," I said, causing his head to snap up. At least he smiled when he saw that it was me. "What are you doing here?"

"You said you'd need coffee after your meeting. How did it go?" Cobb looked so damn good.

His dark hair was tamed perfectly, his dark-brown eyes danced as if he were enjoying my little surprise appearance, and he was wearing a blue T-shirt that fit just perfectly with jeans that probably fit just right as well.

This was almost better than him in his uniform the other night.

"Yeah, but you didn't know what time my meeting was."

He raised an eyebrow. "How did it go? Are you done with the ex-dickhole?" I snorted at the nickname I'd given Owen when I'd met Cobb here on Monday.

"Hopefully. There's no reason for me to have to see him again. It's done."

"That's good."

"It is." But it didn't go unnoticed that he hadn't told me why he was at this coffee house either day that

I'd met him here. Mostly, it was probably none of my business, but talking to him had helped the other day. I would've like to be that for him if he wanted me to be.

"You know…" Cobb leaned across the table on his arms so he wouldn't have to talk as loudly as we were. The place was busy again. "We should meet on purpose. Like for lunch."

I swallowed hard. Talk about meeting the potentially right guy at the wrong time. Cobb was beautiful and seemed to be sweet and caring. Now was just not the right time for me to jump into something.

"As friends?" I asked, cocking my head to the side while trying to get a read on him.

"Yeah, as friends. I can only do friends right now."

The tension in my shoulders released.

Talk about perfect. He could only do friends at the same time I could only do friends.

But the question was: Why could *he* only do friends?

"Perfect," I said with a smile. "Friends it is. When do you want to get lunch?"

CHAPTER 7
COBB

There was something about that woman that I couldn't get out of my mind. The entire time I was thinking of her, I was ignoring texts regarding what I'd come to call my 'New York Problem' and hoping that the lawyer had some information for me. Luckily, he wanted me to come grab coffee with him on Wednesday morning when Monroe happened to be at the courthouse.

With luck, I'd *accidentally* run into her after I was done. I didn't plan on telling anyone else about this situation if I didn't have to.

"Good to see you, Cobb," Manning the lawyer said, reaching his hand out to shake mine. I took it then he sat in the chair across from me and put his cup of coffee on the table.

"You have news?" I asked because that was where my focus was.

His head bobbled from side to side the way it would when someone was trying to say *yes* and *no* at the same time. "I wouldn't say news, exactly. But I've spoken with Hannah's father and their lawyer. She's not interested in a paternity test until the baby is born. Says it could cause complications."

"Could it?"

"My research says yes, but it's extremely unlikely, even in the invasive paternity tests. I plan to petition for a non-invasive paternity test." He took a quick drink then set the cup down with a thud.

"What does that entail?"

"A blood draw from the mother and a cheek swab from the potential father. I assume that won't be an issue."

I raised my hands in the air. "Swab me now."

He chuckled as he pulled a tablet from his bag. "I didn't think you'd protest. Of all the paternity cases I've seen, you are the one most sure you're not the father, and you aren't protesting having to prove it."

I furrowed my brows. "What do you mean?"

"Lots of men *claim* to not be the father. Hell,

they're adamant, but when it comes time to do the testing, they don't want it. They just want them saying they aren't the father to be enough." He looked me directly in the eye. "Which usually means they're the father and are trying to get out of child support. You're not doing that. You're saying you're not, but you're willing to prove it."

"And if it *were* my kid, I wouldn't be trying to get out of anything." Even if I weren't in love with the kid's mother, I'd never turn my back.

"Exactly." He took a deep breath. "The downside is that I'm being told it can't be done this early and really should wait more until after week eight."

"So I've got some waiting to do."

"Yes. But I'll start trying to work the details out with them and if they resist, I'll begin petitioning the court so we're ready when that day comes."

"OK. That sounds like a plan I can live with."

Manning got up from his chair and slid the tablet back in his bag at the same time. Then he patted me on the shoulder. "Don't worry. It won't be long and we'll get this handled. Be glad it hasn't it the press."

"I am." Because then everyone would know and by everyone, I meant Monroe. Her being in the dark about this was exactly what I wanted. Even if we were only friends.

Sitting in that same spot was where she found me maybe ten minutes later.

"Lunch, Cobb?" she asked again because I'd zoned out. "You said you wanted to eat. When?"

"How about now?" I glanced at my phone and saw that it was late morning, but I had to get to the park soon. I wasn't pitching today, so my schedule was a little different. "It'll be early, but I'm hungry."

"Yeah," she said, giving me a sweet smile. "I could eat."

After deciding where to go, Monroe said she'd ridden with her dad again this morning, so we headed to my car and I drove us to the restaurant. This really good sandwich place not far from the field. Best sandwiches around.

Once we'd ordered, we took our lunch to a booth in the corner that wasn't likely to get a lot of attention.

"So is your issue over?" I asked her, knowing she'd realize I meant the whole *damaging the car* thing.

"Yep. Dad paid the damages but says I have to pay him back. Papa would probably be happy to pay for it himself but knows Dad won't budge on this. It's fine."

"So your dad's a lawyer. What does your papa do?" I shifted in the seat because those words sounded weird coming out of my mouth. I'd never called anyone 'Papa' in my life.

She snickered. "He makes furniture. The pieces are pretty popular."

"So I would've heard of him?" I took a big bite of my sandwich because I was starving. Earlier when I'd said I was hungry, I'd downplayed it.

She shrugged. "Maybe. Christopher Bryan is the name he designs under."

My eyes widened slightly. "I think the coffee table in my mom's living room is his."

"She should give it back, then." Monroe snickered at her little joke. "But that's actually awesome. He still does all the designs but only works on the custom pieces for people who request him specifically."

"You mean he makes them?" I asked. She nodded. "With his bare hands?"

She furrowed her brows. "I think he wears gloves a lot of time." Then she cracked a smile. Those jokes might've been awful, but damn, I loved the look on her face as she made them. "Yes. He used to make all of them, but as the business grew, he had to bring artisans in."

"Wow." I sat back. "That's impressive."

"Says the professional baseball pitcher."

Now I chuckled and waved my hand in the air as if what I did was nothing in comparison. "That's a heavy dose of nepotism," I told her. "My dad played, and my grandpa owns the team. It was more the inevitability of the pro baseball player conveyor belt."

She set her sandwich down and popped a BBQ chip into her mouth. "What would you do if you didn't play baseball?"

"I don't know." It was the most honest answer I could give. "I wasn't really ever allowed to think about anything other than baseball."

She bit the inside of her mouth, as if she were trying not to say something, and her blue eyes wouldn't meet mine.

"What?" I asked. When she didn't answer, I said, "We're friends, right? You should be able to say anything."

"Yeah." She scrunched up her nose. "It's not really my place, though."

"I'm asking."

Monroe sighed and now looked me in the eye.

"I was thinking that's a little sad. It sounds like you didn't have a choice."

"Don't get me wrong," I assured her. "I love this game. It's what I would've wanted to do, anyway. The conveyor belt just didn't leave me a decent relationship with my dad. He was hard as fuck on all of us."

"Well, that's worse." She threw her hands in the air. "I can't imagine not being close with my dads."

Now I chuckled. If only she had met my dad… Though that wasn't something I really wanted. "I don't think I'd be close to him either way. He's not exactly warm and fuzzy."

"Still…"

We ate in silence for a couple of minutes before I asked my next question. "Are you adopted? I mean, I figured you are and would already know, given how everything works."

She snickered. "Yes, I know that my dads combined aren't both my biological parents, but I'm only half adopted." Now that I couldn't figure out. "My dad is my biological father. Papa adopted me. They used a surrogate I know almost nothing about."

"So you never met your mom?"

Monroe scowled and the change in her face was

marked. Normally, she appeared to be a completely docile, cuddly little animal. But now she looked like a feral badger about to strike. "She isn't my mom," she snapped. "I don't have a mom. The surrogate helped my dads have a family, which they wanted. It wasn't even her egg. They used a donor."

"Hey." I reached out, setting my hand on top of hers gently. "I'm sorry. I didn't mean anything by it. I don't know how all of that works."

Her face softened and she sighed. "It's OK. I might be a little oversensitive."

"You're not. I should be more careful."

At least after that, we were able to go back to the normal conversation we'd been having before I'd put my foot in my mouth.

Once we'd finished eating, I took the tray to the trash, then we headed to the door, which I held open for her.

"Take you home?" I asked as we walked.

"Yeah. You have to go to work, right?" She looked up at me, squinting in the sunlight.

"In a bit."

When we got to her house, she invited me inside.

Her apartment wasn't large, but it felt bigger than it was. The open-floor plan and light colors probably did that. The kitchen had stainless steel appliances and the only thing separating it from the living room was the couch acting like a divider.

Monroe slipped off her shoes at the door, so I did the same thing, though she didn't ask. It was only fair to assume she didn't want people to wear shoes in the house.

"This is it." She put her arms out and swung around. "Not big, but big enough for me. Oh, the bathroom is there." She pointed to the only door I saw in the hallway. "And of course my bedroom at the end of the hall."

"It's cute."

"I like it. And the price is right." We both chuckled, given that she'd told me her dads didn't charge her rent. "I want to show you something." My stomach tightened, knowing that there were many things I would love to see, but my brain made sure to push that urge away. "You can sit down. I'll be right back."

Monroe hurried down her small hallway, her flowy skirt brushing against the backs of her thighs. It took all of my willpower to pull my eyes away from her and go to the couch as she'd suggested. Monroe was back in a flash, dropped onto the couch next to me and turned with her legs folded beneath her. That damn skirt spread out and raised up her thighs like it was mocking me.

"What's that?" I asked about the things in her hand.

"My mugshots." She grinned. "I thought you'd like to see them."

"Are you serious?" I asked. She nodded emphatically. "How many times have you been arrested?"

She swallowed hard and pushed a piece of her hair behind her ear. "Four, including this last one."

"Damn, girl."

She rolled her eyes at me. "I was taught that when you really believe in something, you stand up for it."

"Did they mean get arrested?"

She snorted. "No. Probably not."

"Good thing your dad's a lawyer."

"That's true."

Monroe reached out to hand me the next picture and the one after. In each one, one corner of her mouth was slightly raised in what might be considered a smirk. It didn't look intentional, more like it was a picture and normally, you'd smile for a picture, but here she wasn't supposed to. That was the best way I could describe the look. She was trying not to smile.

"But I know that I need to be more careful. I graduate in a year and will be looking for jobs. Dad says it'll be difficult if I keep getting arrested. It's why he was so adamant that I not have this one on my record."

My eyes widened in surprise. I didn't know that not having a record was an option. "No record?"

She nodded. "The prosecutor dropped the charges if I pay restitution. Dad paid it today. Now I have to pay him back."

"Does that annoy you?" I asked, still trying to figure out their family dynamic. "That you have to pay it back?"

"Not at all. I caused the damage. I should pay for it. Dad just won't let me pay for it out of my savings. He wants me to earn it and I can see his point."

"You have a good relationship with them?" I passed the photos back to her, though I was tempted to keep one of them. She was so fucking cute in each one that the urge was strong.

"The best, I think." She leaned back against the arm of the couch, but her bare legs were still there and the move pulled her skirt higher on her thighs. Nothing inappropriate, but fuck, did I wish it were. "Asher and Reana say it's unnaturally close, but I think that's just because they have more overbearing parents. They couldn't wait to get out of their houses while I love living here, knowing that I just have to go through that door and my dads are on the other side."

"Asher and Reana?" I knew neither of them was someone she was in a relationship with because she wasn't in one right now. Given that the ex-asshole was her last almost-relationship, according to her. Still, Asher was a name that could go for either a man or a woman and to say I was curious was a serious fucking under-statement.

"My best friends. We've known each other forever. Asher... She's kind of more on the wild side and Reana is far more conservative, I guess is the right word."

"Where do you fall?"

She shrugged. "Somewhere in between."

I pulled my phone out to glance at the time and realized it was later than I'd thought it would be. Though I wasn't pitching today, I had to get to the field to do my off-day regimen. Ice the arm, dip in the ice tub, toss the ball—no pitches—just some-thing to keep my muscles working and warm, then a short bull pen session. I'd already skipped my workout this morning because of the meeting. I'd probably do one later.

I sighed. "I have to get to the field."

Her eyes widened as she unfolded her legs and swung them off the couch. "Of course. I didn't mean to keep you here too long."

I reached out to grab her wrist as she stood up. "You didn't. I just have to get going." An idea came to mind just then and I wet my lips. "Do you want to go to the game?"

"Absolutely." He answer was instant.

"I'll have my sister get you a ticket and pick you up. Is that OK? I know you haven't met her."

"That's fine with me, but I can also drive."

I was already shaking my head before she'd finished. "If she picks you up, I can bring you home. I want to hear what you thought about the game. I'm not playing, of course, but I'll be there."

She furrowed her brows as if she were trying to figure out whether what I'd just said made sense or not. "Yeah, that's fine. Give her my number so she can text me."

"I will." I headed to the door and slipped my shoes on then sat on the bench she had there to tie them. "I'd take you with me now, but it's hours until game time and you'd be bored out of your mind."

"No problem. Gives me time to change."

Once I was on my feet again, the last thing I wanted to do was leave and I was suddenly cursing the universe for making me meet Monroe now when neither of us was in a place to be anything more than friends. I gently placed my arm on her bicep and said, "I'll see you later, then."

"Bye, Cobb."

Then I had to go.

As soon as I was to my car, I called my sister.

"You want something," she answered.

"How do you know?" I said with laughter in my voice as I pulled away from Monroe's house.

"Because all of you only text me. When you call, I know it's a big favor, so what is it?" Growing up with us meant that Camden knew us all too well and was completely accurate in her assessment.

"Can you pick someone up for the game tonight?" I asked, getting myself out of Monroe's neighborhood to head to the field.

"I can, but who? Also, you didn't ask if I was *going* to the game tonight." In my head I could see the pout on her face. She'd tried to use that since we'd been kids.

"I assumed, you're right. Are you?"

"Yes. But that's not the point."

I sighed. "Camden. Please. Can you pick someone up for the game?"

"I already said I could. As long as it's not some disgusting friend from high school I hated." There'd been more than one of those, given that most of my friends had been on the baseball team and Camden hated any baseball players she wasn't related to.

"It's not. Her name is Monroe Phillips. I'll send you the address and her number so you can text her if you need to."

Her breath caught when I'd said *her*. "A woman?" she asked suspiciously. "How in the hell did I become the go-between in my brothers' relationships? Who is she? How long have you been seeing her?"

"First, you've always helped us out when it came to some things, mostly to do with the game. Getting a ticket, making sure Everly knew where to go. Oh, yeah. The brothers talk," I said. She giggled into the phone. "It's not like that, though. We're friends. I met her the other day."

"Uh-huh." The suspicion was still there. As if I couldn't have a friend who was a woman. "You like her?"

"Clearly. I'm not friends with people I don't like." But that wasn't going to fly with her.

"You know that's not what I meant. You *like* her."

Now I sighed. "It doesn't matter, Camden. I've got shit going on and so does she. We're friends. We're going to remain just friends." Even if everything about Monroe was pulling me in. I'd be the best fucking friend she'd ever had.

"You guys are so stupid."

Now, that was probably true in general, but Camden knew everything that was going on with me. She might not have known what was going on with Monroe and honestly, I probably didn't know everything, either.

It just couldn't work right now.

No matter how much I was starting to want that to be wrong.

CHAPTER 8
MONROE

*J*ust friends fucking sucked.

Cobb wanted me to come to the game. He'd asked me. Normally, I would've thought that meant something other than he wanted to be friends, but we were both clear on that.

I liked him, but being friends would have to be enough.

Not to mention it seemed like he had more reason to not want to date than I did, though he never told me what that reason might've been.

For now, I focused on getting ready for the game he'd invited me to. I pulled my hair into a higher ponytail so that it wouldn't be lying on my back. Summer was warm in Michigan and tonight was no exception. Then I changed into a pair of jean shorts and the only Kalamazoo Knights T-shirt I owned. My dads had bought for me when I'd gone to a game with them last year because they'd been wearing their Knights T-shirts and said that I couldn't be the odd man out. I tucked the front of the shirt into my shorts and let the back hang out then pulled on some no-show socks and Converse tennis shoes.

We hadn't discussed a time that his sister was going to pick me up, so I wanted to be ready early.

Then I waited.

I'd never met his sister, so as I sat on the arm of the couch, my leg bounced with excitement. This would be fun.

I'd started getting ready at four and around five-thirty, my phone dinged with a text.

I'm Camden, it read. *Here to take you to the game. Did you want me to come to the door or would you rather come out?*

I quickly typed that I'd be out in just a moment then grabbed my crossbody and hurried out the door.

A blue car sat at the curb in front of our house where Cobb had parked earlier. Maybe not parking in the driveway was a family trait, but in this case, we were just going to leave, anyway. There was someone in the back seat of her car, which made me unsure where to sit. With the passenger seat open, I decided to go there.

"Hi!" The woman driving smiled widely at me. "I'm Camden." She had the most beautiful shade of brown hair—chestnut, maybe—and kind, hazel eyes.

"Monroe," I greeted her.

"In the back seat is Everly. She's my brother Urban's girlfriend and is joining us at the game today."

"Nice to meet you," I told the woman behind Camden. Everly had golden-blonde hair that was pulled away from her face and bright-green eyes that looked like that had gold specks in them. "Thanks for picking me up."

"Not a problem."

"Your brother wanted to drive me home after the game, but I have no idea why." Then I sighed and rolled my eyes. "Actually, he said he wanted to hear my take on the game. Or something like that."

Camden and Everly both laughed under their breaths. "Do you like baseball?" Everly asked.

I turned slightly so that I'd be sort of facing her. "It's fine. My dads are huge baseball fans, so I've been to some games and know some things, but I wouldn't call myself a diehard."

"I knew nothing about baseball beyond the fact that you use a bat," Everly told me. "I'm picking it up a little here and there, but it drives Urban crazy that I have no idea what he's saying when he talks about the game."

"He's desperate for her to learn," Camden offered as we came to a stop at a light. "If your dads are diehards, have they met Cobb yet?" I shook my head. "You should make sure they meet. Cobb is one of the best in the league. Probably will get a Cy Young award this year." Her hazel eyes looked over at me. "That means he's really good."

I snickered because I had a feeling that she was going to explain a lot of things as the night progressed.

We talked about Everly's and my lack of knowledge the rest of the way to the park. Camden, of course, knew everything, it seemed, when it came to baseball. Of course, she had brothers playing and she said her father was headed to the Hall of Fame, too. She'd grown up with it, so it made sense.

When we got out of the car in the parking garage, Camden, Everly, and I met at the trunk and

I followed Camden's lead as to where to go. I'd never been in this lot before.

"I can see why my brother likes you," she said. "You're easy to talk to. Like we just did a twenty-minute drive and I feel like we're friends."

"Me too," Everly agreed.

We stepped out into the sun that had passed over the crest and would fully set before the game was over, so I pulled my sunglasses out of my purse and put them in place.

"He doesn't like me."

Camden stopped and turned to me, pulling her sunglasses down her nose so that I could see her eyes. "He asked me to bring you here. He likes you."

Right. "Yeah. Sorry. As a friend, sure. I thought you meant something else."

A slow smile pushed her cheeks up. "I did, but we'll say as a friend." Then she turned and continued on her way with me scrambling after her as Everly snickered.

"No, seriously," I said. "I have the worst taste in men."

"Same, sister." Everly pumped her arm in the air.

"Cobb and I are just friends. He said that's what he wanted too."

Camden slowed down so that she could walk between Everly and me. "I know he did. He has… things going on right now that I'd bet my entire inheritance he'd want taken care of before dating again. I didn't mean you two are something more, just that he likes you. I know my brothers."

Suddenly I was searching my memory for how many brothers she actually had. The wiki had listed them but for the life of me, I couldn't call it up. Everly was dating one of them and that was everything I knew at this moment.

"Why do you have the worst taste in men?" Everly asked while Camden showed her phone to the man at the door.

This wasn't the normal entrance at all. The crowd was down on the corner and we were the only ones at this door.

Quickly, I gave Everly the Spark Notes version of events with Owen. That relationship hadn't even really been one and he was hellbent on revenge right now because I'd hurt his precious car. However, the fact that he was saying and doing what he had been showed that I had terrible taste.

"Is that the only asshole?" Camden asked. I

nodded. "Then that's not bad taste. Though I think anyone who would willingly be in a relationship with a professional athlete has something seriously wrong with them, my brothers are decent enough."

"Hey!" Everly protested while giving her a shove.

"How many brothers do you have? I'm an only child," I explained. "I can't remember what the internet told me about your family or if you have any that don't play."

"Four."

"Four? Good lord."

She snickered. "I know. And all four play baseball. On this team. They'll all be here today."

I stopped walking. It took the women only a couple of seconds to realize I wasn't still with them. "What?"

"Yeah. My dad's psychotic plan has finally come to fruition. All the boys are on this team. Cobb is a pitcher, as you know."

"Urban plays first base," Everly added.

"Silas is on second and Brooks is a catcher."

My eyebrows were sky high as I listened to them. "None of them liked the same position?" It was a dumb question, but the only one I could think of.

Camden shook her head. "It wasn't allowed."

There were so many more questions swirling around in my head, but now wasn't the time or the place.

"To comment on your claim that those of us in a relationship with a ballplayer are crazy," Everly began, talking to Camden, "the Briggs men have a way about them. I didn't want to fall for Urban. He made it impossible not to."

Camden shook her head. "I think I just threw up in my mouth." Which caused the three of us to burst out into a fit of giggles.

I liked these women and before the night was over, I'd make sure I had Everly's phone number so that we could all talk more.

Once we were in our seats, I asked, "Are all of your brothers in relationships?"

"No." Camden focused on the field where the team was stretching. "Urban is with Everly and I'm pretty sure Godzilla himself couldn't tear my brother away."

"He better not." Everly raised her hand slightly and it took me a moment to realize that she was motioning to someone who looked like a waiter. "I need a drink. Anyone want anything?"

"I'll take a water," I told her and Camden agreed. Three waters would be on their way.

"They have waiters?" I asked.

"In this area," she told me. That was when I realized we must've been in VIP or something. We were very close to the field, on the left side of the dugout by third base.

"Then Silas is with Amity and we love her to death. I've known her since I was a kid. Her brother was Silas's best friend. But Brooks is single."

It didn't go unnoticed that she hadn't mentioned Cobb. "And Cobb is too, right?"

She glanced over at me quickly then looked out over the field again. "Yeah, of course. And Cobb."

"So did they all become baseball players because your dad was one?" I asked. Cobb had made mention of the situation, which made me think that there was more to the story.

"Like playing the positions they do wasn't a choice, playing also wasn't a choice," Camden explained. "But you should ask Cobb about it. I don't want to spill stories he doesn't want spilled."

Yeah. That made sense, but now every scenario I could come up with played out in my mind. I'd definitely ask Cobb about it.

Right then, the Knights began jogging toward their dugout, which wasn't far from where we were. Some of them grabbed mitts and headed out onto the field while I was just hoping for a glimpse of Cobb.

My wish came true moments later when he glanced over and gave me a head nod. I raised my hand in a small wave and noticed that the palms were sweaty. I blamed the heat, but I didn't really think it was the heat.

It was hard to watch the game when Cobb was right there, hanging his arms over the railing of the dugout with a guy beside him. They'd talk to each other with almost every play and it was there that I realized just how nice baseball pants were.

Men talked about yoga pants and sundresses, but women really should've been talking more about baseball pants.

CHAPTER 9
MONROE

"Come on." Everly pulled on my arm so I'd stand. "We'll go down to wait for them."

No one questioned Camden, Everly, and me about why we were anywhere. I assumed that this was a lot like a concert, where you had to have a special pass to get anywhere. When I glanced at Camden, I realized she *did* have a special pass hanging around her neck.

Answered my own question.

"I usually wait for him here." Everly stopped several feet from a door. "If you wait right outside the door, then everyone passes by. It's weird."

As the players began trickling out, that made sense. There were a lot of them and I wouldn't necessarily want every one looking at me the way Everly had described.

Then a man who looked a lot like Cobb came out, glancing around, seeing us then coming our way. He slid a hand around Everly's waist then leaned down to kiss her.

"Hey, baby," he said, then he looked up, like he'd just noticed that Camden and I were standing there. This was Urban Briggs, Everly's boyfriend. With as similar as they were, I was concerned I wouldn't be able to keep them all straight.

"This is Monroe," she told him, pointing at me. "Cobb's... friend."

"Hey." He reached his hand out for me to shake and I did. His hands were large like Cobb's but meatier, if that made sense, and definitely felt like he could crush mine without thinking about it. "Nice to meet you."

"You, too," I squeaked out. There was nowhere in my imagination that I'd even considered I'd be meeting more of Cobb's family tonight other than the sister he'd said would pick me up.

Then more guys came out and I met Silas then Brooks, who had the widest shoulders of the bunch. They greeted me but didn't offer a hand to shake.

Finally, Cobb came over to us and slid in beside

me. "Fuck. Did any of you even shower?" he asked his brothers. All their dark hair was slightly damp, so they must have.

"Yes," Brooks told him. "We all did. Because we actually played."

Camden snorted on the other side of me.

Cobb held his hands up. "It's not my fault I'm only allowed every fifth game."

"Fuckin' pitchers," Silas said with a grin. "Have to baby the shit out of them."

Cobb shook his head. "Blame the game for pitchers to be the most important part of the team."

The rest of them groaned, making me believe this wasn't the first time these things had been said. They were brothers giving each other a hard time. I might not have had siblings, but I knew people who did.

"Are you all done comparing dick sizes?" Camden asked over the noise. All at once, the guys' tone changed. Gone was the playful verbal sparring to be replaced with disgusted noises in the backs of their throats.

Cobb was the first to speak. "I could go my whole life without hearing you say the word 'dick' like that."

She cocked her head to the side and said, "Like what?"

"Without *you're being a* before it," Cobb explained. The guys chuckled.

"Whatever." She took two steps away from us backward. "I've delivered the lady—*ladies* to you like I said I would and now I'm going to go." She turned so that her back was to us and began to make her way out of the park, but then called over her shoulder, "I'll text you, Monroe. We'll get together and do something."

I didn't have time to respond before she turned a corner and was out of sight.

"Let's go," Cobb said quieter so that I was probably the only one to hear him. His hand was on my lower back as he led me away from the group but then dropped once we were away from any crowd.

Damn. I missed the pressure of his hand on my back.

It wasn't until we were inside his car that I said, "I'm sorry you lost."

He shrugged. "They played better. Not sure what was going on with the third baseman, but it's fine. You win some. You lose some."

"Still. It was fun to watch."

He raised an eyebrow and glanced at me before focusing on the road again. "Yeah?"

"Yeah. Camden explained some things as they came up. I knew a little, but I think I learned a few things today."

"That's good. It's the best sport around."

Quickly, I wet my lips and twisted my fingers together in my lap. "Camden said to ask you why you became a baseball player. All she said was that it wasn't a choice, so I think it's because your dad is one."

"It is because my dad was one, but he put us on the baseball conveyor belt early. He had a plan that all of his kids were going to go pro and create some fucked-up baseball dynasty."

"And you all did?"

"I guess. But Camden fucked his plan up because she's a girl and can't go pro. At least not yet."

That gave me something to think about.

"Are you hungry?" I asked when he pulled up to my house.

"Always."

"I have some delicious leftover lasagna that I was going to heat up tonight and if you're really nice to me, I'll share it."

Cobb smirked then ran his tongue over his bottom lip. "I'll be *very* nice to you."

The words had so much double meaning that goosebumps skittered across my skin and a chill ran up my spine.

I'd bet he could be very nice. Too bad that even if I could be convinced for more with him, he wouldn't be. That had been made clear. Even his sister knew he wouldn't get into a relationship right now.

I brought Cobb into my apartment and pulled the lasagna out of the fridge so that I could heat it in the microwave. Once it was done, I cut the giant portion Papa had sent for me in two, my piece being much smaller.

"Normally, I'd do a vegetable with this," I told him. "But it's too late for that."

"This smells amazing," he said as he sat down at the island in my kitchen. I moved my plate over so that I was kitty-corner to him, standing with my bare feet against the cool tile. I'd gotten rid of my shoes and socks as soon as we'd come through the door.

Cobb took one bite, closed his eyes for a second, and said, "Holy shit, that's good. Did you make this?"

I shook my head. "Papa did. He makes the pasta from scratch and the sauce. It's the best I've ever had."

"Me too."

And we were able to eat that lasagna while talking more about the game. Of course, he had insight into all of it that I couldn't dream of having. He'd been learning his whole life, but I was a quick a study. When I told him I always thought the bat would vibrate out of their hands when they hit a hundred-mile-an-hour ball, he said he'd show me how to hold it so it wouldn't.

"I'm not sure I want to get near anyone throwing a hundred-mile-an-hour ball anywhere near my head."

He chuckled. "I wouldn't let it hit you. Hell, I can be the one pitching to guarantee it wouldn't hit you."

"It's a hundred miles an hour," I countered. It seemed like a death defying proposition to me. I didn't like to be put in situations where I had to defy death.

"I wouldn't throw it that hard," he promised. Cobb wouldn't let me get hurt. That much I could be sure of but I still hoped that this was all hypothetical.

"I should go," he said once we'd finished putting the dishes in the dishwasher. "Have to meet my brothers for a workout early."

"Do you work out every day?"

"Yes. I normally take November off, but then I get right back to it. In the off season, it's not every day, but during the season, pretty much. There's always something to work on." He moved over to the door and sat down on the bench to put his shoes on. "Listen, we're off tomorrow and after the work-out, we're hitting the pool at my parents' house. My dad's out of town, so we don't have to deal with him. Mom will likely be working, but we're having dinner there. Want to come?"

"To your family thing?" My stomach dropped. That wasn't a friend thing, was it? "I don't think so."

He sighed, then stood and came toward me until he was so close, I had to fold my arms under my breasts to keep from reaching out and touching him. "Listen, it's not a big deal. I like spending time with you and really, I haven't reached out to any of my old friends since I've been back." He wet his lips and put his hands on his hips, like he had to figure out what to do with them. "I like hanging out with you. I think I've already said that."

As I thought about that and the fact that I'd only known him a matter of days but was already attached, I ran my tongue quickly over my suddenly dry bottom lip to think about how I wanted to answer. It didn't take much thinking because of course I wanted to spend time with him.

"We leave on a road trip on Friday," he added and that meant I wouldn't get to hang out with him.

So… "Yeah. I'll come. You said pool. Bring a bathing suit?"

His jaw tensed. "Yeah." I nodded, but then he…

Quickly pushed his hand into my hair and his lips pressed against mine. The surprise took me off guard, causing a delay in my response. Cobb was so much taller than me that he had to lean over, making it so that the only thing surrounding me was him.

Which should've been to push him away. He was going to ruin a perfectly good friendship here…

Instead, I slid my hands up his hard chest until my fingertips met the skin of his neck. He wrapped his arms around my waist and pulled me closer. His mouth moved against mine and he tasted like the pasta sauce we'd both just eaten. His tongue caressed my lips until I parted them.

When his tongue touched mine, it was like reality set back in and I brought that to an end by stepping away. The heat of my cheeks rivaled the sun.

"Why would you do that?" I demanded, though the only thing I wanted was to do it again. "You said friends, Cobb. You only wanted to be friends. *Could* only be friends."

He closed his eyes and let out a long sigh. "You're right. I'm sorry, Monroe. It won't happen again."

"But why?"

"You were standing there looking very kissable and... I don't know. The intrusive thoughts won out. I'm sorry." He raised his arms out to the side then let them fall. "It won't happen again. I promise. Please still come to the pool."

I swallowed hard. "I'll see you tomorrow." Because right now, I was irritated. Here I was trying to avoid making a stupid decision and he'd kissed me.

He'd said it'd never happen again.

And that was the last thing I wanted.

CHAPTER 10
COBB

*I*t's rare that we got a day off.

Scratch that. We got one or two a month that were actual days off with nothing to do for the team. There were other days we traveled and while we weren't playing, that doesn't really constitute a day off.

But today we'd be at my parents' house because that was where the pool was. My parents had an amazing backyard, perfect for entertaining and now that all of us were on the same team, we'd be putting it to use more.

Fuck. We were all on the same team. Something none of us had wanted to happen. It wasn't the *playing together* part. It was being on the Knights. That fucking stung and I was supposed to be the holdout. Then the scandal—or potential scandal—had come along and fucked me.

At least I'd get to spend time with Monroe before the road trip.

Now, I knew how it looked when she pulled up in her blue Prius. My brothers had their girlfriends with them—minus Brooks because he didn't have one. And me. I also was single, but it sure as fuck didn't look it as I watched Monroe swing a bag over her shoulder as Camden hurried toward her from the garage.

Yeah. My sister was here too. Her best friend, Harlowe, would probably show up at some point if she wasn't working at the bar.

"Hi." Monroe's smile was brighter than the sun. She was wearing a dress, but it didn't look like a normal dress. It looked more like the coverup that Camden was wearing since she had her bathing suit underneath. It hung from her, giving no glimpse of what was beneath. Monroe's strawberry-blonde hair was pulled up in a bun, with little tendrils falling in some spots. Her look was effortless.

"Hey," I told her, but I couldn't take my eyes off her. If she was wearing makeup, I couldn't tell, though her lips shone like she'd just put gloss on.

The rest of her looked so fucking natural and it was working for me.

I'd kissed her last night, which was wrong and I shouldn't have done it. Still, it was replaying in my head over and over right now, making it all I could think about. It didn't matter that I desperately wanted to do it again. I was in a situation that made that impossible and given her last ex-asshole, I didn't want to be another bad decision for her.

Monroe narrowed her eyes and cocked her head to the side. Her lips parted like she was about to say something, but before she could, my sister threaded her arm through Monroe's.

"OK, well... I'm going to go introduce your *friend* to anyone she hasn't already met because it doesn't seem like you're going to." Then she pulled her away.

Why had she emphasized 'friend' like that? I didn't know and I wouldn't ask, at least not right now.

Camden pulled Monroe through the house to the sliding doors then outside to where everyone else was. When I stepped out behind them, my sister jumped into introducing Monroe to Amity since she was the only one Monroe hadn't met yet. Silas and Amity were on one of the lounge chairs, her between his legs, back to his chest. Urban was sitting at the table with Everly beside him. Everly, she'd already met. Urban just waved. And our oldest brother, Brooks, was at the grill, already cooking.

"Mom said she'd be home later," Brooks told me once the greetings were done. Camden went over to the outdoor fridge and grabbed Monroe a diet pop. Something I should've thought of.

"At least Dad's out of town," I countered as I opened the bottle of water Brooks tossed at me.

It was an off day, but none of us drank much alcohol in general, let alone during the season. Maybe a beer here or there, but not often. It was better to keep our bodies in top shape rather than try to recover. Recovery was a bitch.

"So, do none of you get along with your dad?" Monroe asked. It was brave of her to broach the subject with people she didn't really know.

Camden raised her hand. "I do."

Urban snorted. "Do you?"

"For the most part," she countered. "We butt heads, sure, but he didn't have me on the conveyor belt, so we're mostly fine." That much was true.

"What do you do, Monroe?" Amity asked. "School? Work?"

"I have one year of college left and I live at home with my dads." Brooks raised his eyebrows at me and I knew exactly what he was thinking. Dads, plural. That would mean a lot of fatherly oversight, but I shook my head. Monroe and I weren't like that. "They have what's called a mother-in-law suite, so it's like my own apartment. Separate entrance." She shrugged. "I like living close to them."

"What are you majoring in?"

"Political science, but I might go to law school." She glanced at me then back at Amity. "One of my dads is a lawyer and I wouldn't follow his footsteps because he's a criminal lawyer, but I'd like to do something that would make a difference. Maybe environmental law."

Everly snapped her fingers. "Or maybe you could do criminal law but work for something like the ACLU or the law poverty center. Help people who couldn't afford to have a lawyer."

"That's true." It sounded like something Monroe was seriously considering. "I hadn't thought of that. I've been arrested a couple of times." Amity's mouth dropped open. "Just for protesting. Not leaving when I was told to." Her cheeks pinked up. "Except this last time and I'm lucky. I have my dad, but a lot of people don't."

A silence fell over the group, the rest of them probably wondering why she'd been arrested this last time. To avoid that, I told my brothers, "Her other dad is Christopher Bryan."

The sound of surprise filled the air. "Seriously?" Brooks asked. I nodded. "I have one of his dinner tables. Mom gave it to me when I moved out. I think she felt a little bad that I got drafted right to the Knights. Dad wouldn't shut up about it."

I snorted. That sounded like our dad. "Yeah. Mom has his coffee table in the living room. I think that one is actually his."

"What's that mean?"

Monroe took the time to explain with as popular as her dad's furniture had become, he had woodworkers that build most of it. Still his design, just not his hands that made it. That wasn't the case when he'd first started.

"I could tell you," she said. "If you show it to me, I can tell you for sure if he made it himself."

"Come with me." I used two fingers to motion for her to follow then once inside, I took her hand and led her to the living room. "Here it is."

A small smile formed on her lips, then she went

over to it and ran her hand across the table. "This is one of his older pieces." Then she got down on the floor and shimmied her body under the table. The coverup she was wearing moved up her thighs.

I tried to look away but couldn't make myself. Her skin looked so soft, making my hands ache for her.

Good thing I was leaving on a road trip tomorrow.

"Can you come down here?" Her voice brought me back to reality.

"Yeah." There was no way I could slide all the way under the table like she had. I was far too big to get under there.

Turned out, it didn't matter. She was sideways by the time I'd gotten down there, so my head was very close to hers.

"Do you see this emblem?" She ran her hand over the marking that I'd never seen until now because I'd never been under the coffee table before.

"I see it." But I barely looked at it. My focus was on Monroe.

"He only puts this emblem on the ones he actually built." She brought her eyes down to me. "The furniture that he didn't build himself has a different emblem."

"That's good to know," I said quietly while the pull to kiss her again worked hard, but I had to work harder.

"Food's ready." My sister's voice snapped me out of whatever trance Monroe had over me.

I hopped to my feet while Monroe slid out, then I offered her a hand to help her up. We went back out to join everyone else. It wasn't lunchtime, nor was it quite dinnertime. My brothers, their girl-friends, Camden, and I had been here quite a while already, but Monroe had some things she had to do this morning and I thought it involved the job she needed to get to pay her dad back for the damages to that asshole's car.

Obviously, he was an asshole, given that Monroe was sweet as hell, so if she'd felt the need to retaliate like that, there had to have been a reason.

Brooks had made burgers on the grill while Silas, Urban, and I brought things out from the fridge. Had we made those side dishes? No. But we knew where they were. Once we all had our plates made, we found spots at the table. Not surprisingly, Urban and Silas sat next to their women while I had Monroe on one side and Camden on the other.

"Cam, is Harlowe coming?" Brooks asked. "I can make more if I need to."

Camden snorted. "She doesn't eat that much, but no. She's working."

"She's always working," Silas said and it was true.

Harlowe's family owned a bar and grill close to the ball field and it was always busy. But from what I'd been told, she'd been working there so much more than either of her parents. Camden had said she just wanted to buy it from them but didn't have the money yet.

"Speaking of..." I turned to Monroe. "The stuff you had to do this morning. Was it about that job?"

She nodded then swallowed quickly. "Yeah. Papa wanted to introduce me. It's all set. I'll start training soon. It's not a lot of hours, but I should be able to pay Dad back."

"Pay him back for what?" Camden bit off the end of a pickle more aggressively than she needed to.

Monroe put her burger down and wet her lips before taking a long drink. "My dad paid the damages as restitution on the last time I was arrested, but he wants me to work to pay him back. No taking any money out of savings for it, he said."

"But you're an adult. Can't you do it, anyway?"

My sister got my best glare. She was prying too far with Monroe. "I could," she said. "But I understand what he's doing and why, so I'm going to do it his way."

"What'd you do?"

Monroe sunk her teeth into her bottom lip and her cheeks pinked up. "Threw a brick through someone's car window." She took a breath. "And kicked the side of his car that might've left a dent, but he says the glass ripped his leather seats and there's no way."

"Mm-hmm." Camden nodded as if she totally understood. "An ex? Was he a baseball player? Because I'm telling you, baseball players are the worst."

Monroe's laughter filled the air and it was music to my ears. "No. Not a baseball player and only sort of an ex. We dated a few times a while ago, but he kept popping up, asking me out again—"

"I didn't know that."

She shrugged. "No reason for you to. But he's one of those guys who gets mad when he gets turned down. Anyway, on this particular day, he was harassing a friend of mine for being out with his boyfriend and I… snapped, I guess. My dads are gay, obviously, so it hit a sore spot. I couldn't challenge him physically. The guy's too big, so I did the next thing I thought of."

Camden reached around me with her hand up for a high-five, which Monroe gave her. "I'm with you, sister. That guy deserved even more. I bet it felt good."

Instead of agreeing, Monroe just shrugged. "But all the other times I was arrested were for protests. I swear. This was a one-time momentary lapse."

I sat back and put my arm on the back of the chair as I watched her continue talking to my family, knowing that what she'd done had been brave and not a lapse at all.

But it was also why she questioned her taste in men and didn't want a relationship at this point. Though I'd been the one to insist that we could only be friends. In her situation, she could decide a man was an exception to the rule that last fucker made her think was true and change her mind. I couldn't change my mind until my New York situation was over.

After we'd cleaned up, we all dove into the pool.

But before that, the moment Monroe took her coverup off... I thought I'd drool. She was curvy in all the right places with more smooth skin on display than I thought I could handle. She wore a blue bikini that was just the right amount of sexy.

"Careful." Brooks slapped my back harder than necessary. "If you start to drool, I'll make sure everyone knows."

I shook my head. "I don't know what you're talking about."

He chuckled. "Of course you don't. Except that you're looking at that woman like she's a steak perfectly prepared for you to eat."

My jaw tightened when he said the word *eat* because sinking my teeth into Monroe was abso-lutely on my bucket list.

"You know I'm not looking for anything."

He sighed. "Yeah. I do and I know why. You could just explain it to her."

"So she can think I'm trying to get out of taking care of my own kid?"

"It's not your kid."

"I know that. But the last guy she dated I bet she didn't think was a fucking homophobe, right?

She doesn't trust her own judgment because of him. What are the chances she'd believe me?"

"Better than you think, I bet." He took a step closer. "But you're not denying that you want her."

"I don't." That didn't even sound convincing to my own ears.

"Right." He laughed again then patted my shoulder. "You're completely fucked."

Then he jogged off and hopped into the water.

We were in the pool—all of us—for quite some time. Until we felt the first raindrops.

"I didn't even know it was supposed to rain," Camden whined. Neither had I.

The entire group was back under the canopy, and the women had put their coverups on over their bikinis, right as the sky opened up to dump a massive amount of rain. This wasn't a gentle sprinkle. It was pouring.

I grabbed a bottle of water and handed one to Monroe as our entire group stood under the canopy.

"I love the rain," Everly said. "Maybe not this much, but there's something calming about it."

That was when Monroe looked over at me with a sly grin. "I like the rain, too." She might've been responding to Everly, but she was talking to me.

Then she shrugged as I lifted my bottle to my mouth. Suddenly, I was very thirsty. "I'm already wet."

I snorted and the water sprayed out as Monroe ran out into the rain. She threw her arms out and spun in a circle like she had when I'd first dropped her off at her house. She lifted her chin so that the rain was falling directly onto her face.

"That looks like fun," Amity said as we watched her. Then suddenly, all of the women ran out to join her and squeals of laughter filled the air.

When Monroe waved me out, Brooks slapped me on the back. "You're fucked, Brother."

The problem was... he wasn't wrong.

CHAPTER 11
COBB

*N*ot kissing Monroe again last night might've been the hardest thing I'd ever done.

I walked her out to her car, told her to let me know she got home safely. All of that and it sure as fuck felt like boyfriend shit.

If only I didn't have the New York situation hanging over my head. It wouldn't be fair to bring her into that—if she'd even come. I had a feeling that there was more to the ex-asshole story than she was letting on, considering she'd said that they'd barely dated, yet he'd fucked her confidence when it came to picking men. Or was it that he hadn't been her first bad decision, according to her? In my eyes, she was blameless.

After packing my bag and heading to the field, I realized that I hadn't mentioned how long we'd be gone. This was only a three-game series, so I'd be back in a couple of days.

Why did I want her to know that? I hadn't told any of my other friends.

But I couldn't kid myself anymore that Monroe was like any other friends, even if we'd only known each other a matter of days. It wasn't like I'd fallen in love with her, but the problem was that I could. Easily.

That was a problem for me.

Once I was on the bus, I pulled my phone out to text her and there was already one waiting from her.

Have fun on your trip. See you in a few days.

After telling her that I would, I realized that she must've looked at the schedule to know it'd only be a few days, but a jolt ran through me at the fact that it seemed a given we'd see each other.

"Texting Monroe?" Brooks asked as he dropped into the seat next to me.

The way the team worked, we took a team bus to the airport, where we got on the team plane. Then a team bus took us to our hotel or the park or wherever we were going. There were so many rules on road trips. For example, wives, girlfriends, and partners couldn't even stay at the same hotel. Except Amity because she was part of the team. As the assistant travel secretary, she sometimes went on the road with the team, but it wasn't like she could share a room with Silas.

"She texted me to have a good trip. That's it." I slowly slid my phone back into my pocket to fight the temptation to keep texting.

"I like her," he told me. "She seems great. Where'd you meet her?"

I sighed. As my big brother, he wasn't going to let this go. *Fuck*. People talked about how tough it must've been for Camden to grow up with four older brothers, but no one said shit about being the youngest brother.

"Coffee place across from the courthouse."

"Something to do with her being arrested?" He shook his head. "I cannot imagine that woman as a criminal."

I snorted. "She showed me all of her mugshots." He laughed out loud. "But I see what you're saying."

"She just looks like such a good girl. I seriously can't picture it, but hey." He bumped my shoulder with his. "At least they were for good causes, right?"

"Sure." I didn't care why she'd been arrested at this point, but he wasn't wrong. She wasn't out there doing shit for no reason. Monroe was actually trying to make the world a better place.

"So what's going on with the two of you?"

The bus pulled away from the corner and we were on our way.

"We're friends."

He snorted. "You almost choked to death on water because she said she was already wet last night."

"No, I didn't." Yes, I had. "She'd been in the pool."

Now he sighed and sounded so much like a disappointed dad. "Cobb, come on. It's me you're talking to. Why are you fighting this with her? You clearly want her. You look at her like she's the sweetest piece of cake. I know you too well for you to bullshit me."

As I pinched the bridge of my nose and closed my eyes, I knew that he wasn't going to drop it. "Because of the New York thing. I don't want to bring anyone else into that with me. If it gets out, you guys will already be involved. No room for anyone else."

"Please." He scoffed. "All of us know it's not

true and wouldn't give a shit. I mean, you're the kid who carried a baby doll around. Pretending to feed it, change its diaper. You did that until you were fourteen."

I rolled my eyes. "I was five." Not even close to fourteen. By fourteen, I'd been thinking about girls and when I'd lose my virginity and how to do that without creating a real baby.

He snickered because he knew damn well it hadn't been age fourteen. "What I'm saying is that you're the most nurturing of the bunch. We all know you wouldn't do this. Now if it was me... there'd be questions. Babies freak me out and I don't know what to do with them."

"You'd figure it out and I can't imagine any of us leaving a woman pregnant with one of our kids on her own."

"No. That's true." He quickly wet his lips. "I'm just saying not to let this bullshit hold up any part of your life. Sure, it means you're here and I can't say I'm sad about that. I like all of us on the same team and now that you're here, it's unlikely you'll be leaving unless you decide to become a free agent when your contract expires."

"I could do that." Though I didn't really want

to. There were too many unknowns with free agency.

"You could." He nodded then looked me in the eye. "But you'd have to stay at the level you are now. No slumps, probably take a pay cut because Mom is going to offer you a fuck ton of money."

"Yeah." And as much as I hated to admit it, I liked us all being on the same team. "I don't know what will happen. I've got time to think about it."

"Besides…" He put one earbud in his ear. "By that point, Monroe will be a factor and I bet you won't want to leave." Then he slipped the second one in and closed his eyes so that no matter what I said, he wouldn't hear it or know that I was saying it.

Asshole.

The flight was short, the hotel nice, but we were whisked off to the ballpark pretty much as soon as we'd gotten checked in. We had a game to prepare for. Well, they did. I had a workout to do. I was set to pitch tomorrow, which meant I needed to do a practice run today. Make sure my mechanics were on par.

At this point, it was mostly muscle memory.

I did everything I was supposed to then had lunch with my brothers and headed to the game.

We'd snack a little before the game, or they would because I wasn't playing, to make sure they had the energy. We'd have a late dinner. That was just how it was on game days.

The game was... rough. It wasn't that the other team was playing harder, it was that we were both playing the hardest and were pretty evenly matched. In the end, they won with a two-run walk-off.

Rough, but their fans loved it.

After showering, we got on the bus back to the hotel, then I ordered room service and decided to call Monroe while I waited.

I was thinking about her too much and shouldn't have called her at all.

Friendship was hard. Or at least it was when you desperately wanted to get that friend naked.

So maybe don't call her. Fuck, I didn't know.

My head was tight and starting to hurt.

If I called her, maybe she'd only take it as a friendship thing. Could she take it as anything else? Of course, but I didn't think she would. She wasn't showing any signs of wanting anything more than friendship, that was clear.

Not calling her didn't say anything. She probably wasn't expecting it, but fuck, I wanted to.

So I would.

Right after I'd let room service in with my food. I had the guy set it on the table, then once he was gone, I sat down, propped my phone up on the vase of flowers, and chose Monroe's contact for a video call.

Her beautiful freckled face answered on the second ring.

"Hey," she answered, her strawberry-blonde ponytail swaying from left to right, which meant she was moving.

"Hey. You busy?"

She flopped down onto her stomach on a bed. "Nope. Just at home. Nothing exciting. How was your game?"

"Fine. We lost."

Her brows pinched together. "Sorry."

"It's fine," I said with a shrug. "Can't win them all."

"That's true." She reached back and tugged on whatever was holding her hair, allowing those waves to cascade around her. I paused the bite of chicken halfway to my mouth. The corners of her mouth turned up. Clearly, she'd noticed.

So I took the damn bite. As she spoke, she moved so that she was sitting up with her back against the headboard. I'd been to her place, but not into her bedroom, so I couldn't know for sure that was hers. But she'd said she was at home, so it had to be.

She squinted her eyes at the phone. "Are you eating?"

"Yeah." I chewed some more then swallowed. "Just got back to the hotel and ordered room service."

"Doesn't that get expensive?"

"We get a per diem on the road, but I don't think about it much." Then I paused. "That's such a rich kid thing to say."

She shrugged. "It's fine. I understand, anyway. It's not like I grew up worrying about food or safety."

"Is that why you protest?"

She took a deep breath and her eyes stayed on the phone before she answered. "No one's ever asked me that yet. I come from a place of privilege and want to make the world a better place in the ways that I can. I don't get the same treatment as others and I want to use that for good."

"What do you mean, you don't get the same treatment?" I continued to eat as we talked.

"Well, I was arrested the second time with a

woman my age who happened to not look like me. I was out that night, but she was there for days. When I found out, I asked my dad to help. He did and got her out as well as the charges dropped. But it shouldn't take her happening to know someone with a lawyer dad."

She was right. It shouldn't.

Now, all of us donated to charity, but it felt like there was more I could have been doing. Maybe that was something I'd have Monroe help me with. But later.

"Does your dad do pro bono a lot?"

She shook her head. "He does some, but he's in high demand and there isn't always time." Then she sighed. "What about you? What are you doing tonight?"

I pointed the fork at my plate. "This."

"What?" She giggled. "Aren't you like a young, hot, baseball stud phenomenon? Aren't you supposed to be clubbing it up? Going home with a bunch of women?"

Now it was my turn to laugh. She really had no idea what this life was like. "No," I said through my laughter. Once I'd calmed down, I continued. "Not at all. Even if I were, I wouldn't. That's not my thing. I mean, I am young and a baseball phenomenon—though I'd never call myself that— and if you say I'm hot, I'll take it." Her cheeks pinked up when she realized she had said that. "But clubbing? No. I don't even like parties." And the last one I'd been to had bitten me in the ass. "A bunch of women? No thanks."

She rolled her eyes playfully. "You're in your prime. If not now, when?"

"We have rules on the road. We have to be in the hotel at a certain time... all that shit. But seriously, ask my brothers or Camden. None of that was ever me."

"Rules?" She sat up straighter. "What kind of rules?"

I went on to explain to her that we were required to travel with the team, be in the hotel at a certain time, partners of any kind weren't allowed in the same hotel. All of that. She held on to every word that I was saying until she sighed then poked at her phone.

"What's wrong?"

Then she groaned. "Nothing. I just have to block another number."

I furrowed my brows. "What are you talking about?"

She nibbled on the corner of her mouth and

blinked a whole bunch of times. If she didn't want to tell me, she didn't have to, but I very much wanted to know.

"I sometimes get these random texts and they have to be from Owen, but they aren't from his number."

"Owen?"

She groaned and dropped her head back. "Ex-dickhead."

My stomach tightened and my fingers held the fork more firmly.

"Why's he texting you?"

"You don't want to know."

My eyes narrowed on her. "I assure you, I very much want to know." It was hard to keep the concern and anger out of my voice. I had no right to feel protective of her or possessive, yet here I was feeling both.

"Fine." She didn't sound that happy. "In this case, he wants me to know that paying for the damage wasn't enough."

My jaw tightened. "What does it actually say?"

She rolled her eyes again but tapped at the phone. "'You might think Daddy can buy your way out of all of your trouble, but I assure you, that's not the case.'" She dropped back against the pillow again. "OK?"

"Not **OK**. That sounds threatening. What's up with this guy? Why didn't you date him longer?"

"For the same reason I threw the brick at his car," she said. We held in a stare-down. I'd wait her out all night if I had to. There had to have been more. I mean sure, who would want someone like him, especially when she had two dads, but that didn't make sense for him to keep texting. "Fine. He was a controlling asshole. We were on a date—though we only went on, like, four or five—and I saw someone I know. A guy. He freaked out in the car that I was talking to another man while out with him. Or talking to another man at all."

"Is that all?" I asked through clenched teeth.

"He had a three-date rule."

"What the fuck is that?"

"If you don't have sex with him on the third date, you're not worth his time. For some reason, he made an exception for me because we went out on more than three and I never had sex with him, but after the third date, it was mentioned each time."

"Fucking Christ." I sat back, suddenly no longer hungry as the rage flowing through me was enough to feed me. "That's bullshit."

"Exactly. And why I stopped seeing him."

"Yeah, but if he's not leaving you alone, that's worrisome. Do you report these texts?"

"Report what?" She snapped to sitting up straight. "They aren't threatening. I block the number and move on."

I swallowed hard. Was it my place to push this? Yes, because I fucking cared about her. "You should at least tell your dads."

Her eyes widened and she snapped her fingers. "Did I tell you that I'm bringing my dads to the next home game?" she asked, changing the subject. "I have to see if Dad has his season tickets. He usually gives away the ones he doesn't think he's going to attend, but if not, I'll buy some. You don't have to meet them or anything, I—"

"Don't buy any. If he doesn't have them, I'll get some from my mom." But I knew what she'd done there. She'd changed the subject because she didn't want me to push her on telling her dads.

I'd let it go for now.

"Your mom?"

"Yeah," I told her. "She always has tickets held back until game day to give to people, business associates, giveaways, charities, whatever. Just let me know if he has them."

"I will." A small, satisfied smile appeared. She was probably patting herself on the back for getting us off the topic of the ex-dickhead and how I'd let it go. But I wouldn't forget about it.

"I won't be pitching that game. I pitch tomorrow, which is Saturday, so I won't again until our Friday game. It's every fifth game."

"Got it. We're still coming, though."

I chuckled. Clearly, I wasn't the draw or at least not the only one.

"Can I ask you something, Cobb?"

The way she'd said my name shot right to my dick. I wasn't proud of it. "Of course."

"Why'd you kiss me?"

All hope I had of that being ignored washed away. "I don't know," I told her honestly. "I wanted to and it was a serious lapse in judgment. It won't happen again."

Her shoulders fell and I couldn't tell if it was in relief or disappointment. Relief, I would think. She didn't want me kissing her and I'd crossed that boundary.

"Are you sure?" she asked quietly.

"Yeah. I'm sure."

But fuck, I didn't want to be.

CHAPTER 12
MONROE

*C*obb was sure he'd made a mistake kissing me. He was positive it wouldn't happen again.

And I was... disappointed?

I bit my lips together in a thin line and fell back onto my bed then pushed my legs out straight.

Where the disappointment had come from, I had no idea. I didn't want him to kiss me or... well, do anything a friend wouldn't do.

Owen had scared me off. Made me think that I didn't know how to pick a guy.

Shit. That wasn't exactly true. I'd had an off feeling about that man after the second date and it'd just gotten worse from there.

It was more his reaction to me dating again that

I worried about. I wanted him firmly out of my life before I brought someone else into it where they'd have to deal with him. It was annoying, but I liked to have my proverbial house in order.

What most people didn't know... or really anyone besides Owen and me was that there was more to the story about the night I'd thrown the brick through his window. Yes, I'd thrown it because of the reason that I'd said. He *had* been harassing my friend.

It was more about the *why* he'd been doing it.

Owen had known it'd be the quickest way under my skin and earlier that night, I'd gotten under his. Completely unintentionally. I'd been talking to a guy in the club. Scratch that, *he*'d been talking to *me*. I hadn't even known Owen was there, but when he saw it, the moment I'd stepped away from my group to use the restroom, he'd grabbed my arm and pulled me into the restroom.

He hadn't hurt me, but it was made clear that he'd make my life a living hell whenever I was with someone.

I didn't even think that he wanted me. It was more he didn't like being told *no*. Oh, and I was just a rich bitch. His family didn't have money and that clearly put a huge chip on his shoulder.

But when Cobb had kissed me… something inside had woken right up.

Something that I'd forgotten about.

It'd been so long since I'd had sex. Over a year because that was the last time I'd been in a relationship. I'd dated three guys since then, but we hadn't clicked and I wanted to click with someone who was going to see my naked body.

As Asher would say, *"It's been too long since I've had that good D."*

Even thinking that made me roll my eyes.

But Cobb's kiss had been amazing. It had taken everything in me to pull away when all I'd wanted to do was melt into his arms.

My skin grew hot thinking about it. The fluttering in my chest was like the soft wave of a butterfly taking leisurely flight. The skin on my arm was sensitive to my own touch.

All of this was from simply *thinking* about Cobb. What would it be like for him to actually touch me?

I trailed my fingertips up my arm, over my collarbone, then down my chest between my breasts and the hard nipples on top.

It'd been a while since I'd taken care of my needs myself. Maybe it was time.

My finger had just pushed under the elastic in my sleep shorts when the bell rang.

Who the hell could that be?

I hopped up, grabbed my phone, then hurried out to the living room. While the app opened, I made sure my door was locked. There was good security out at the garage door as well, but something made me double-check.

It was eleven-thirty at night. My dads were out of town for the night and they wouldn't be outside ringing the doorbell that had been rigged to my apartment even if they were here. Luckily, it came with a doorbell camera, so I didn't have to go out there or open any doors.

Fuuuuuck.

Owen's face appeared on the night vision camera.

"What are you doing here?" I asked.

"Just want to talk to you." His words slurred together. The telltale mark of the fact that he'd been drinking.

I groaned silently. "Not tonight, Owen. It's late."

"You're not asleep. Let me in."

"I'm not letting you in." I hurried to the door that connected my apartment to the house and opened it. If he came through the door on the garage, I'd hurry into the house and lock that door. I'd never shown anyone the door that goes directly into my dads' house. It looked like a closet door and would take him a while to figure out. He'd think I was hiding in my apartment.

But then I could get away from him and call the police.

None of which I actually wanted to do.

"Monroe… Precious Marilyn…" He sang while I cringed. He knew I'd hated it when he'd decided to come up with the nickname 'Marilyn' for me. He thought he was so clever.

"Go away, Owen."

His jaw tightened. "I'm not going away. You might think that because you're some rich bitch, you can tell me what to do. You can't. Daddy paying for the damage isn't enough. You tried to humiliate me. It's only fair I return the favor."

"I'm calling the police," I told him, not knowing if that would escalate things or make him go away.

"I'm not going anywhere."

"You're drunk," I told him. "Go sleep it off and leave me alone. I'm not opening the door."

He reared back and punched the door. Luckily,

Dad had gotten reinforced steel and it hurt his hand more than it hurt the door.

"Fuck," he yelled into the night then turned back to the camera. "You're not getting off that easy, Little Marilyn."

Cringing at his comment, I had to be thankful that he at least backed away. I waited, holding my breath until I heard a car start up and an engine get quieter. Another check of my camera showed that no one else was out there. He hadn't parked in range of the camera, unfortunately.

I let out a breath and fell back against the wall then slid down until my butt hit the floor. Then I held the corner of my phone to my head just trying to breathe.

It wasn't until that point that I let myself realize that I'd been scared. Of course I had. My heart was pounding and my hands were shaking. After several deep breaths, I was feeling closer to normal.

But my hands were still shaking. Calling my dads was out. They didn't know how agro Owen had been with me and I didn't want them to. Also, they so rarely went away together that I wouldn't be the interruption to their night.

The only thing I could think that would calm me down was to talk to Cobb. But I couldn't. It was like eleven-thirty here, ten-thirty where he was, and I knew he'd be going to bed because he had to pitch tomorrow. He said he always tried to go to bed early the night before he pitched, and besides, his body was on our time.

Still, reaching out to him would help, I thought. If I called Asher or Reana or both, they'd answer and want to talk about it and ask a million questions. If Cobb was asleep, I wouldn't hear from him until tomorrow.

I know you're probably asleep and that's why I'm sending this to you instead of calling. I have to say it in some way. I just had one of the scariest moments of my life. Sleep might not be for me tonight, but the only thing I could think of to calm me down was reaching out to you.

Maybe I'll delete this before you read it.

Then I hit *send*, knowing I had time to delete it before he read it.

Or thinking I had time because no sooner had I sent it was my phone ringing and it was him.

I closed my eyes and took a deep breath.

"Hello."

"Are you all right?" he asked without any small talk beforehand.

"Yeah. I'm fine." But my voice wavered slightly and he'd catch it.

"What happened? Your text freaked me out."

I sighed. "I'm sorry. I only sent it to you because I thought you'd be asleep."

"I was in bed but not asleep." Something moved on his end. "Why would you want me to be asleep?"

"So I wouldn't have to explain or answer questions," I told him honestly. There was no reason to not be honest at this point. "I thought I'd delete it in a minute and you'd never see it."

He sighed. "I'm glad I saw it. What happened?"

"See? This is what I meant about talking about it."

"Monroe." He wasn't going to let me get away that easily.

So I took a deep breath and said, "Ex-dickhead showed up at my door. Freaked me out, but I'm fine. It's fine."

"*What?*" His voice was low, which made it sound more dangerous.

"Yeah. It's fine. He was drunk."

"What'd he want?"

There wasn't any easy way to explain that, now was there. So the question became: How truthful was I going to be with Cobb?

Completely truthful was the right answer if we were going to remain friends.

So I told him everything that had happened and even told him the whole story about the night at the bar before I'd thrown that brick. Cobb remained silent the entire time until I'd finished.

"So he's why you don't want to date right now?" he asked, as if the point needed clarification.

"Yeah." I shrugged, though he wouldn't see it. "I figured I'd let this die down. Bringing someone else into this mess wouldn't be right."

He snorted, but it wasn't in humor. "I think that would be for the guy to decide."

I was already shaking my head. "No way. I don't want someone stepping in to fight my battles. I can handle this. Every woman everywhere has had to deal with a guy who doesn't like the word *no*."

"Can you go stay with your dads tonight?" he asked.

"What?"

"I know your apartment is already connected, but I'd feel better if you were closer to them. I know this isn't about how I'd feel, but can you?"

"It'd be letting that asshole chase me out of my own place." Which I didn't want to do. "Besides, my dads are out of town for the night."

There was a noise—it almost sounded like someone had choked—then he said, "So you're there by yourself?"

"Yup. And I'm fine. He didn't get in."

"Did he *try* to?" he almost yelled and I realized that I'd left out that tidbit.

"I don't know that he was trying to, but he did punch the door. Said he wanted in to talk to me."

"Will you go stay at my apartment?" he asked. "No one knows we're friends and no one would know where I lived even if they did. You'd be safer. Just for tonight."

"I'm fine here, Cobb. I'm sorry I sent that text."

"I'm not," he snapped, then he sighed. "I'm sorry for that. Please?"

I snickered. "The part of no one knowing where you live means that *I* don't know where you live."

"I'll send you the address."

"I won't be able to get in," I countered. "Do you have a little turtle with a key hidden in it?"

He was silent for a few seconds, then said, "No. I'll call my sister. She'll meet you there. Or better yet, she'll come get you so you don't have to go alone."

My eyes widened and I hopped to my feet. "It's

almost midnight, Cobb. That's a huge inconvenience."

"I promise it won't be," he said. "Please."

But then my phone began making noise and it was him trying to video call me. So I shook my head and answered. Now that I could see him, it'd be much harder to keep saying *no*.

Maybe that was the plan. Maybe he wanted to woo me in with the bare, muscular chest I could now see. Though I'd seen it yesterday at the pool. His skin was golden but looked so soft.

"Monroe," he said, like he'd already been talking.

"Sorry." Hopefully, he hadn't noticed my ogling. And at least he didn't know that I'd been thinking about him when I'd almost touched myself earlier.

"Will you go to my apartment? Please?" Those big, dark eyes drooped with concern.

"Yeah," I finally said. "OK."

He slowly closed his eyes, as if this were the biggest relief of his life. "Good. I'll get a hold of Camden. She'll let you know when she's on her way. You go pack a bag and please call me when you're inside my apartment with the door locked."

"I'll text you," I assured him. He was about to protest. "I'll text you, Cobb. I'm not calling you and keeping you awake any longer. If you suck tomorrow, it won't be because of me."

Now he laughed. "I won't suck tomorrow and I won't sleep until I know you're there."

"OK." There wasn't much else to say and he had to call his sister.

While he did that, I packed a small overnight bag with anything I might need and a change of clothes for tomorrow. Fifteen minutes later, my phone dinged with a text from Camden telling me she was there. Then the doorbell rang.

I pulled up the video feed to make sure and she was there with a large man I didn't recognize not far behind her. He wasn't looking at my door. He was looking behind him. I grabbed my bag and left my apartment, making sure to lock everything behind me.

Stepping out into the dark night was eerie. At least I wasn't alone and thankfully, Cobb had sent Camden because I didn't think I could've gotten myself to leave on my own.

"You ready?" she asked. I nodded but glanced at the man with her. "Oh, this is my best friend, Harlowe's, cousin. He's just here to make sure your ex isn't hanging around."

"I don't think he is."

She threaded her arm through mine to begin walking us to her car in the driveway. "I don't, either, but just in case." She got me into the passenger seat then called out, "Thanks!?" Which must've been for her best friend's cousin, then she was in the car behind the steering wheel. Right away, she started the car and backed out of the driveway.

"This is seriously overkill," I muttered.

"What?" she asked, sounding as chipper as she had every other time I'd talked to her. Tonight she had her brown hair in two braids that sat below her shoulders against her chest. At least she didn't look like she'd been out for the night.

"I said this is overkill. Did your brother tell you what happened?" I asked. She nodded. "So you know it was nothing. I didn't need a chauffeur and a cousin bodyguard." Because I hated feeling like I was helpless or needed this kind of help.

"Whoa. I'm only here to let you into Cobb's apartment. I have a key. Though I did think I'd see about staying the night with you like a little slumber party. We could call Everly and Harlowe. See if they want to join. But we don't have to."

God, this made me sound like such a bitch.

Here she was taking time out of her night to help me and I wasn't exactly being grateful.

"I'm sorry," I told her. "That was me being a bitch when you're going out of your way to help me."

She shrugged. "I understand, but I'm helping my brother. You didn't call me, but you know you could have, right?"

I hadn't wanted to call anyone and, at the time, reaching out to Cobb was the only thing I thought would calm my nerves. He made me feel safe in a way that Camden wouldn't have. Neither would Asher and Reana. They would've hurried over to stay with me, of course, but it wasn't the same.

I nodded. "Why not Amity?" I asked. She furrowed her brows. "You said we could call Everly and Harlowe but didn't mention Amity."

"Oh." She smiled widely. "She's on this road trip, so she'd miss out."

Camden pulled us into the parking lot of a high-rise apartment building. The place was new and nice and stretched forever into the sky. Though it was dark, so who knew how tall it really was?

"OK," she said once we'd gotten to his apartment on a higher floor. "Let's go eat all of my brother's food."

I snickered. It was such a sister thing to say. She locked the door behind us and flipped on a light.

Cobb's apartment wasn't how I'd pictured it. The place was modern and much cleaner than I would've expected.

"My brothers are pretty neat," Camden said as if she could read my mind. "They aren't really messy. Never have been, but they also have a cleaning lady and this apartment actually belongs to the team. Cobb hasn't found his own place yet. This used to be Urban's but he's staying with Everly until his place is finished."

She went on to explain that the team had a couple of apartments in this building where someone who'd been traded last minute could stay until they found their own place because a player could be in one city one day and the next be playing in a game on the other side of the country. It was hard to move your whole life in a single day.

"You better call my brother," she reminded me.

"Right." I pulled my phone from my pocket, flipped on the camera and took a picture of myself with his living room in the background as proof of life—or in this case, proof of location. Then I typed out that I was here and the door was locked.

Good, he sent back. *Don't be afraid to send me a*

picture of you in my bed before you go to sleep. Or better yet, when first wake up.

I snickered as I sent him a crazy-faced emoji.

If I didn't know better, I would've said that Cobb was flirting. But he wouldn't flirt with me because kissing me had been a mistake that wasn't going to happen again.

He'd made sure I understood that.

CHAPTER 13
COBB

*T*here was nothing like coming home after a road trip. Even a short one.

I dropped my bag by the door and half-expected Monroe to still be there, but she wasn't. Honestly, I probably should've known she wouldn't be. She'd stayed the one night, but not the other and I knew this because I'd talked to her every night after the game. There wasn't a reason for me to convince her to stay here after the first night because her dads were home. Which meant the argument that she'd be alone wasn't going to fly.

Likely, she wouldn't have let it fly, anyway.

Monroe was one of the most independent women I knew. She wasn't going to stay away from her home because some guy had spooked her. She was far less worried about him than I was.

Yet something inside me swelled knowing that she'd been in my space. My bed. Even if I hadn't been there.

Brooks had been right at my parents' house.

I was fucked when it came to Monroe.

Still, I wouldn't bring her into my mess, so anything I might want to do would have to wait.

While I stood in the living room, noticing a folded blanket and pillow on the end of the couch, the lock that I'd just locked on the door disengaged. I turned to see who the fuck was coming into my apartment, knowing there were very few options.

Monroe walked through, her hair pulled up into a messy bun and she was wearing what looked like pajama shorts and a tank top.

She startled, gasped, and took a step back. "Oh, shit." She placed a hand over her heart, like she thought it was going to pound out of her chest. "I didn't think you'd be back yet."

"We left right after the game. Which is why I didn't call. Figured I'd call when I got home."

She shut the door and came farther into the apartment. "You're not required to call me every day."

I furrowed my brows. "I know I'm not required. I like to, but if you don't want me to——"

"If I didn't want to talk to you, I wouldn't answer the phone." She crossed her arms under her breasts. "I forgot my phone charger here when I left yesterday. Didn't realize it until the middle of the night and didn't want to come then." She took a deep breath. "I forgot about it until I needed it about twenty minutes ago. My phone died, so I wouldn't have been able to answer. But I would've wanted to."

Monroe came over closer to me then held out her hand. It took me an embarrassingly long time to figure out that she was holding my key up for me. "Camden gave it to me," she said. "In case I needed to come back last night. I told her not to, but…"

"I'm glad she did. Keep it."

Her eyes widened, turning into two little teacup saucers, and her lips parted, reminding me of exactly what those lips had felt like against mine. If I wasn't careful, I'd be sporting a raging hard-on right there in front of her.

"In case you need to escape here again," I explained and even lied to myself as to that being the reason I wanted her to keep it. That was part of it, but not the whole story. Over the last week, I'd been falling for her more and more.

"It's fine, Cobb." She pushed her hand closer to me, but I folded my arms over my chest, which reminded me that I was still in dress clothes. Another requirement of travel. The rules didn't say you had to wear a suit, but jackets were required for the plane. It was a whole thing.

"Seriously, Monroe." She watched as I gently pushed her hand back closer to her. "It'd make me feel better. If you ever need it. You have it."

She sighed but closed her fingers around the key.

"What else are you doing tonight?" I asked.

She waved her hands in front of her body. "I'm in my pajamas. My plan was to grab my charger, plug in my phone, and watch a movie. I lead a very exciting life."

Sounded exciting to me. "Why don't we watch a movie here?" It wasn't late by any part of the imagination. Around nine. Tomorrow was a night game that I wasn't pitching, so I didn't even have to be to the park until after lunch.

Monroe was going to say *no*. That was for sure. But then she nodded, went over to the door to kick her shoes off, and came back to the couch.

"'I'll grab us some drinks," I told her as I headed to the kitchen. "Want anything to eat?"

"No thanks. If you have a diet pop, I'll take that. Otherwise, water, please."

Out of the fridge, I took a diet pop and a water because that was what I wanted and came back to the couch. "You get the movie up that you want to watch while I go change."

She didn't have time to protest. I grabbed my bag and headed for my bedroom.

The room hadn't been touched, as far as I could tell. Between that and the things I'd seen on the chair in the living room, Monroe hadn't sleep here the other day.

"Sorry about leaving the pillow and blanket in here when I left. Camden got them for me, but I didn't know from where."

"It's fine."

"She put hers away before I was really up. Said she had to meet someone and I didn't want to keep her."

After moving my bottle of water to the end table, I sat on the couch and put my feet on the coffee table. "Monroe, it's fine. I don't care that they're there."

She worried her bottom lip before looking up

sheepishly. "Would you care if I used the blanket while we watch the movie?"

"No." I snickered. "Are you cold?" The air was kept down because I ran warm and she was standing there in not a lot of clothing.

"Not really. I just like to be cozy."

So I shrugged. "Mind sharing?" I knew exactly what I was doing. Torturing myself by having her so close knowing that she didn't want me the way I wanted her and even if she did, I still couldn't have her.

"Sharing is caring."

Monroe set her drink on the table then grabbed the blanket before spreading it out over us. She tucked the material under her chin so her head was the only part of her still visible, but that didn't deter my dick from become half-hard.

Once we were settled, I turned the movie on.

That movie became another and I'd sit there watching with her all night if she let me. Watching her watch so intently was now my new favorite pastime. Her lips parted at certain parts, her breathing quickened at the love scene, and she ran her tongue over her bottom lip and I didn't think she realized she was doing it.

I had to stop watching her. If I didn't, I'd be a stalker and I'd never get this erection to go down.

Then her head hit my shoulder. Leaning forward, I saw that she was asleep, holding that pop in her hand. Carefully, I took it from her and put it on the end table next to me. Then I adjusted my body so that I was at an angle, which caused her to fall into my side.

Was it wrong? I didn't think so. It was for her comfort. That had to be better than her head at a ninety-degree angle on my shoulder, which probably felt like a rock.

That didn't help the erection at all.

We stayed like that. Or rather, I kept us there like that until I knew I had to get to bed. We had a game tomorrow. Luckily, I wasn't pitching. Otherwise, I would've already been up way too late. Sleep was the most important part of being an athlete. Without it, we'd play like shit.

"Monroe," I said, gently running the backs of my fingers down her cheek. I'd wanted to touch those freckles the first time I'd seen her. "Monroe."

Her breathing changed, her head moved, forcing her face into my side and then slowly, her eyes opened and she was looking up at me.

"I fell asleep," she said tiredly.

"You did."

Her eyes widened and she bolted upright. "I fell asleep on you. Literally. I'm sorry."

"Nothing to apologize for." Not even the granite erection I'd been sporting for an hour now. "You were tired."

"I didn't sleep much last night."

My stomach clenched as to why that might've been, but I wasn't going to ask now.

She grabbed my phone from the table and brought it to life.

"Oh, my god." She slapped a hand over her face. "You should be asleep, right? You have a game tomorrow."

I shrugged. "I do, but I'm not playing. I have to do my workout and throw some balls. Nothing major."

She blinked three times slowly. "I'll get out of your hair," she said as she pushed the blanket down her legs.

Before she could get up to grab her purse, I wrapped my hand around her wrist. That small touch flooded my body. Her skin was so fucking soft. "It's late. Why don't you stay here?"

A look crossed her face, but I didn't know that one. To me, I would've said it was desire.

"I can't do that, Cobb."

I furrowed my brows. "Why not?" She bit her lips together to indicate that she wasn't going to tell me, so I sighed. "If you leave now, I'm going to follow you home to make sure you get there safely." Even if that dickhead hadn't showed his ugly head again, I felt like the word dickhead applied to that situation.

"There's no reason for you to do that."

"There is." I pushed up to my feet. "It'd make me feel better. You might not need it, but I do."

Fifteen seconds passed between us, both staring at the other in a showdown. If she wanted to leave, I wouldn't keep her here. I wasn't a fucking stalker. But if she insisted on leaving, I'd absolutely follow her home to make sure she got there safely.

"Fine," she finally said, but she didn't sound happy about it. "I'll stay. Your couch is comfortable, anyway." She passed me on her way back to where she'd been sitting.

"What? You mean because you just fell asleep?"

She shook her head, those strawberry waves brushing against her shirt. "I slept on the couch on Friday night."

"Why?" I didn't stop until I was standing in

front of where I'd been sitting. She was in front of where she'd been sitting.

"Where else was I going to sleep?"

"The bed." I pointed toward my room.

"No way. That's your bed. Too personal."

"It's a bed. You've slept in a hotel before, right?" I asked. She nodded. "Same thing."

Her fingers tangled in front of her. "It's not the same to me. I don't know those people."

"Well, you're not sleeping on the couch tonight."

"Yes, I am," she countered.

"You sleep in there. I'll sleep on the couch."

Her eyebrows pinched together. "Not a chance, Cobb. You have a game tomorrow."

As frustrating as this conversation was, I kind of wanted it to go on all night. The way she fought back was a fucking turn-on.

"How about this? We can share the bed."

Her mouth formed an 'O' as she looked up to meet my eyes. "No way."

"There's room for two."

"Do you know how many romantic comedies use the *one bed* trope, Cobb?"

I shook my head. "Sadly, I don't."

"Well, it's a lot and we can't do that."

Biting back a laugh, I told her, "We'll make a board that goes between us. Like the Amish supposedly do." Then I put my hands on her shoulders just to torture myself a little more. "It'll be fine, Monroe. We're both adults. It's not a big deal."

She let out a long breath. "Fine. But I'm not ending up pregnant."

I snorted. That wasn't what I'd expected to come out of her mouth. "Agreed."

Though I didn't tell her that there were ways to do all the things and still not get pregnant. That would've been a little too much and she probably would've run for the hills. And since I had no intention of touching her, anyway, it was best to leave it unsaid.

Monroe came over ready for bed, but I had to brush my teeth and change into to boxer briefs because that was what I slept in. When I came out of the bathroom, she was standing at the foot of the bed. Her gaze jumped to me as her eyes scanned down my body, lingering in some areas more than others.

Luckily, I'd gotten my dick to calm down. I'd considered beating one out before bed to satisfy it but had decided against it. Nothing would satisfy me wanting Monroe other than Monroe. Since that wasn't possible, I'd have to live with it.

"What're you doing?" I asked her as she shifted her weight from one foot to the other. "Why didn't you get into bed?"

"I don't know which side you like."

"I don't care."

She sighed. "Cobb, this is your bed. Where do you usually sleep?"

"Probably the middle, so I can do either side."

She shook her head but went around and climbed into the side across from where I was and every movement had me rethinking the whole *taking care of myself* issue.

Monroe was so fucking beautiful, I could hardly stand it.

Instead, I climbed into the other side of the bed, keeping as much distance between us as possible just so I wouldn't accidentally touch her, but I did roll on my side, facing her. She was on her back staring at the ceiling.

"You all right?" I asked.

Without looking over, she said, "My dads saw the ring camera video." I waited because there had to be more. "Dad wants to file a protection order so Owen will leave me alone. Papa wants to know if there's more that we don't know about. Things I haven't told him that led to me throwing the rock, which pissed him off and led him to my apartment."

My muscles tightened, but thankfully, it was dark and she wouldn't have noticed. "He thinks it's your fault?"

"No." She turned on her side so that she was facing me, leaving an entire chasm between us. "He doesn't think it's my fault. He just thinks that it was an extreme thing for me to do and there had to be more."

"Did you tell them?"

She shook her head softly. "If I do, they'll insist on the order and I don't want to do it."

"Why the fuck not?" It came out more aggressive than I'd meant it to, but I left it hanging out there.

"It's just going to make him mad and probably won't stop it. I just want him to leave me alone. It's not constant. I don't fear for my safety."

I raised my brows. "You don't? Why'd you call me the other night?"

She winced. "I shouldn't have. I was just——"

"Scared, Monroe. You were scared of what he might do at that moment. Getting the order is just for protection. Maybe he'll leave you alone then. This doesn't say anything about you."

"It says that I'm a weak girl who needs her daddy to fight her battles."

"Pft. It does not. If Camden had a guy messing with her like this, she'd have brothers to handle it for her. It doesn't say anything other than people care about you." And I was one of them.

The thing about this situation was that it didn't sound like he was a physically abusive ex or that she really thought he'd do something. He was irritated right now. She was right—he'd probably just go away.

But what if he didn't?

"I'll think about it," she said softly.

"Good."

"Good night, Cobb," she said, her words surrounding me like a blanket.

"Good night, Monroe."

My brother had said that I was fucked when it came to her. I'd agreed in my own head, though I wouldn't say it out loud to anyone and if I told her that I was fucking falling for her, she'd bolt. No question.

But I turned over so I wouldn't be tempted to say the words and tell my problems to fuck off so that I could have her, even though it wouldn't be fair to her.

No. It was only a couple of more weeks before my lawyer could ask for a court order to get that paternity test and it'd all be behind me. Then and only then could I allow myself to consider starting something with Monroe.

She deserved the best and right now, that wasn't me.

CHAPTER 14
MONROE

hy was it so weird being in Cobb's bed? I hadn't stepped foot in his bedroom when I'd been here two nights ago. His sister had slept in his bed then changed the sheets in the morning. Though she'd joked about leaving it so everything would smell like her soap and shampoo to fuck with Cobb. In general and if he brought a woman home.

That was when I'd desperately wanted to know if that was something he did often. She confided that no, he didn't. He usually was a relationship guy, unlike her heathen other brothers. Though now two out of the three were in actual relationships.

My discomfort—if you could call it that—came more from Cobb being here with me.

Looking over and seeing him made my core ache and I had to clench my legs together to get some relief.

Maybe getting the protection order wouldn't be such a bad idea. Maybe that would put Owen in my rearview faster and then I could be honest with myself and with Cobb about what I wanted from him. What I wanted *with* him.

Because even now, I wasn't fully honest with myself. I'd allowed myself to know that I was attracted to him—it wasn't like I could hide it—but beyond that, I kept a trap door shut over those thoughts and feelings.

What good would it do me, though? Cobb told me he could only be friends, too. There was a reason for that. I just didn't know what it was.

After enough time had passed and I clearly wasn't going to get sleep, I slowly took the blanket off me. Cobb was being so good at staying on his side and hadn't made contact with me once.

Thank god. Otherwise, he would've set me on fire and it didn't matter how innocent the touch was, either.

Everything I did was in quarter speed and with purpose. I got my legs over the side of the bed, but as soon as my feet had hit the floor, Cobb said, "Are you leaving?"

My shoulders slumped. I'd thought he'd been asleep. "Just going out to the couch."

He sighed in the darkness. "I'll go, but can you tell me why? I haven't moved."

"I know." Maybe it was the cover of darkness, but suddenly, I felt bold. "Do you want the truth?"

"Of course."

"I can't be in this bed with you. Lying here next to you is too much. It's got my hormones going crazy because you look like... well, *you* and you're a great guy. You've been there for me when you didn't need to be. I feel safe with you, which apparently is something I was lacking and didn't know it."

The light next to his bed clicked on, so I bit my lips together and my cheeks flushed.

It was much easier to say these things in the dark.

"Hormones, huh?"

I rolled my eyes. "I'll just go die now." I turned to hurry out the door, but he suddenly jumped in front of me, causing me to skid to a stop.

"Hang on," he said, holding his hands up as he took a step away. I didn't know if it was his intention, but the movement told me that I could keep going if I wanted to and he wouldn't stop me. "Explain."

I rolled my eyes. "I think I already overexplained and I'd like to go bury myself in a hole right now." It had to be late. I was going to be the reason he got hurt tomorrow. His focus wasn't going to be there.

"So being next to me has your hormones going crazy." He smiled but bit his lips together like he was trying not to. Cocky bastard.

"Move, please." Though he wasn't really in my way.

Cobb stepped aside so that I could continue out to the living room, where the couch would be good enough to wait until the sun came up, then I could leave before he woke.

"All I'm saying," he said to my back, "is that I could help you out with that."

My footsteps stopped and I turned slowly with wide eyes and pinched brows. "What? Are you crazy?"

He shrugged. "Maybe. But I could."

"We're friends, Cobb. We've both been clear that we aren't anything else. We're friends." I sighed. "Unless you're talking about taking me to buy a battery-operated boyfriend, which I'm really not interested in."

He chuckled. "I wasn't, but you shouldn't count poor B.O.B. out."

To hide the embarrassment of this whole thing, I slapped a hand over my face. "I can't believe you just said that."

"We *are* friends." He took a step closer. "But I could be a friend who helps you out. It's not even a hardship like helping you move or driving you to the airport. It'd help me out to." Then he pointed down.

My eyes followed where he was pointing to find a hard cock behind the cotton of his boxer briefs. "I've been dealing with that since you sat down next to me on the couch. Fuck. Probably before that."

Heat fanned out across my chest and up my neck. Normally, I wasn't easily embarrassed by sex talk. I was an open person. This wasn't about the talk, but who was saying it and who he was saying it about.

I cocked my head to the side. "Are you serious right now? I don't know how to take this."

"I'm completely serious."

"Have sex then continue to be friends?" I

confirmed. He nodded. "I've never done that before, Cobb. I don't have one-night stands."

He chuckled. "This wouldn't be that, would it? With one-night stands, you never see the other person again. Hopefully."

Everything in my body screamed at me to jump at him immediately, but my brain wouldn't stop.

I wanted Cobb. Probably had wanted him since I'd seen him in that coffee shop. But would this change things?

"Listen." He stalked toward me, not stopping until he was right there within touching distance. "You said being close to me has you horny." I opened my mouth to dispute that claim, given that those had not been my words. "I know you think you didn't say that, but you did." He pushed his fingers into my hair, cupping my cheek with my palm. That was the moment I knew I'd never be able to hold out. "We don't have to do this. I just wanted you to know it was an option."

Just having him this close had me wet and squeezing my legs together to relieve some of the pressure. It wouldn't be enough. Nothing would be enough without his touch.

My breath quickened as I looked up at him.

How did I say it? *Please fuck me, Cobb?* That wasn't about to come out of my mouth.

Luckily, it didn't need to.

Whatever he saw when he looked at me was enough.

Cobb pressed his lips to mine.

His mouth was wet and hot against mine as he walked me backward toward the bed until my legs hit the mattress and I fell. When my ass hit the bed, Cobb didn't allow our connection to break. He pushed his hands into my hair, cupping each cheek with his large hands. I trailed my finger tips up his bare chest.

Cobb's skin was so smooth and soft over the hard muscles that playing baseball gave him.

Once I was breathless, he pulled back and slowly slid my pajama shirt up my body until he could toss it away over his shoulder. I'd never been self-conscious about my body and that wasn't about to start now but the way he looked hungrily down at me had my stomach squirming.

He looked like a man dying for a taste.

Which if we were doing this, then he probably was but the intensity in his gaze had me feeling... things. Things beyond the sex we were about to have and I couldn't let that happen. I couldn't catch feelings when I knew he couldn't return them.

Instead, I laid back, propping myself on my elbows and bit into my bottom lip. His chest rose quickly and his jaw tightened as his gaze slid down my body.

Without touching any part of me, Cobb leaned slowly in and took one of my nipples into his mouth. I dropped my head back and groaned so he scraped his teeth over the sensitive skin.

"You did that on purpose," he said, his voice deeper than it normally was.

"Did what?"

"But into your bottom lip." His hand trailed up my chest, between my breasts, coming to a stop with a loose grip around my throat. It wasn't choking me. Just resting.

"I mean, of course I bit my bottom lip on purpose. I just didn't know you like that."

"Me either."

He dropped to his knees and ran his big hands up my thighs to push them apart. Then he kissed from my knee until he hit my pajama shorts.

"Well, these are in the way," he said right before yanking them down my legs. Then he did the same with my panties. There was absolutely nothing sexy about those panties. Just cotton bikinis because I like to keep things breathable but that didn't seem to matter.

Then I was completely naked but he still had his boxer briefs on. Not exactly fair but given what I thought he was about to do, I wasn't going to complain.

Cobb shoved a two fingers into his mouth then pulled them out with a pop. Slowly, he worked those fingers into me, watching as he did it. Now that... maybe that made me a little self-conscious.

Watching him was too much. Just him touching me about sent me to that euphoric place we were both chasing. So I laid back, and let myself be in the moment. Shut off my brain and just feel.

When he licked me, my legs tried to clamp shut involuntarily. He used those large, strong hands to push them away so he could continue his work. He sucked my clit into his mouth and ran his tongue over it as he pushed and pulled his fingers.

In no time, my orgasm slammed into me one wave after another, again and again until I didn't think I could take it anymore. Once I came down and my muscles relaxed, Cobb pulled his fingers out of my for the last time, moved to... somewhere then came back. I finally forced one eye open to see him opening a condom package.

Well, it was my turn.

I pushed myself up until I was sitting then looked up at him with a mischievous grin. Once he noticed it, I raised and eyebrow. He blew out a breath and handed the package to me.

After ripping it open, I set it on the head of his cock and slowly, as slowly as I could allow myself to, unrolled it over him.

"You're killing me," he said then growled in his chest.

"That's on purpose, too."

But the moment I got it full on him, he nudged me back and sunk into me. I wasn't even all the way on the bed and neither was he.

Didn't matter. He slammed into me like he couldn't wait another second. We were only like that for a few moments when he pulled out and told me to get up on the bed.

"I was so close," I pouted. He would've been the first to give me a second orgasm.

"I'll get you there."

I wasn't sure if it was a promise, but it sounded like a vow.

With me in the middle of his bed, this time,

Cobb moved slower. Everything was slower, most purposeful. He brought me to the brink again then backed off. I didn't know if it was his goal for me to kill him but if he did that again, I probably would.

"Cobb." It was a warning and a plea but he snickered.

"It's just this one time right?"

I froze. I'd be lying to myself if I denied that this felt more than physical to me. But that was the agreement so I nodded.

"Then I'm going to take my time."

Take his time, he did.

Cobb's tongue pushed into my mouth as he slid in and out of me, slowly, making me want to scream at him to hurry up. But he was right. If we were doing this just this once... helping each other out, as he put it... then I'd be patient.

But then he got impatient and thrust himself into me harder, faster. I thought he was about to lose it and this was going to end without that promised second orgasm but he pulled back and slipped his hand between us. First he touched where were connected and dropped his head to my shoulder. Then he moved his fingers to my clit where it only took three circles for me to come undone.

Which meant he could too.

"Fuck," he muttered with his forehead pressed to mine. Then he kissed the spot his head had been and slowly pulled out of me, holding the condom the way you're supposed to. Not every guy did that or knew to. It was all part of taking care of me.

"Do you want the bathroom first," he asked. I shook my head, unsure if my legs would hold me up just then. "I'll bring a cloth back to clean you up."

"No." I grabbed his arm. "I'll use the bathroom after you."

He nodded then he was gone.

CHAPTER 15
MONROE

*O*nce Cobb was back, I did my thing then got my pajamas on and crawled back into his bed. The lights were off so at least he wouldn't be able to see what I thought was likely written all over my face.

I'd buried any feelings I had for him because neither of us wanted anything more. But this... it showed what could be and that was the best experience of my life. Maybe it wasn't for him but there was no universe where anything would top that.

"Hopefully you can sleep now," he said in the dark.

My eyes were closed and I snorted. "I think I'm halfway there."

If he said anything after that, I didn't hear it.

I snuck out the next morning because looking him in the eye after what we'd done was something I needed to work up to. It wasn't the sex. It was the fact that I now knew that I really wished it had been more than sex.

Since I didn't leave a note or anything, I expected an irritated text from him, but one never came. In fact, I didn't hear from him at all.

Well, shit.

After going home, obsessing about Cobb's hands on me… his mouth… and showering, I did everything I could to waste hours of my time before going into my dads' house to see what the plan was for the game tonight.

"Hello, Fathers," I greeted them. They were both in the kitchen with a cups of coffee in their hands. Dad was wearing khaki shorts and a polo shirt, which was basically his uniform when he wasn't working in the summer. While Papa wore gray shorts with a white T-shirt and a checkered button-down that was open.

They were far more stylish than me, given that I was wearing a pair of jean shorts with a Kalamazoo Knights tank top.

"Hey there, baby." Papa pulled me into his arms and kissed the top of my head, his nose hitting the bun I had painstakingly put my hair in. It was going to be a hot day. "So what's the plan? Game is in a few hours."

I swallowed hard. There was no chance I wasn't going to see Cobb there. "Well, I thought we could eat then head to the game. Tickets are at will call. Cobb wants to hang out after and drive me home, but I might rethink that."

Dad set his coffee cup in the sink. "If you would've told me, I wouldn't have given my seats away."

"I know, but it's last minute. I didn't know I wanted to take you. You'll be so impressed with what I've learned."

Dad narrowed his eyes on me. "So you wouldn't learn for us, but some pitcher comes along and suddenly you love baseball?"

I snorted at the ridiculousness of his statement. "Not *some pitcher*, right? Isn't he the *best*? Aren't I supposed to be savoring seeing him play so that one day I can tell my children that I saw the greatest play? Even if he's not playing today, it would still spark and interest, right?"

Papa laughed loudly. "Not exactly."

Once I'd stopped laughing with him, I said, "I have always had fun with you at games. I've also gone to every game you've ever invited me to. Us going isn't unusual."

"Some guy providing the tickets is," Dad countered.

"OK." I shrugged. "We'll buy tickets instead, but since his mother is the owner of the team, I'd bet these are going to be pretty fantastic."

And that wasn't something either of them could argue with. Instead, they agreed for us to head out to dinner. Dad took us to his favorite non-fancy restaurant where we could get burgers because other than hot dogs, what else said *summer baseball game*?

We were settled and eating, having a good time with lots of laughter, when Dad finally cleared his throat, clearly wanting us to be more serious. "We've talked about it, Monroe, and we don't want you to pay us back for the damages."

"I never wanted you to," Papa clarified, making Dad scowl. "What? I didn't. I may not have said it but I never did." They didn't have the kind of relationship where one backed the other up no matter what when it came to me. I guess they sort of did. Papa made his opinion known but didn't try to go against what Dad said.

"Right." It was hard to not giggle at the unbothered look on Papa's face. "I don't mind paying it back, though." I hadn't actually started at the coffee shop yet. The owner had said he'd meet with the manager to work it out and have the manager call me. It was only one of his locations so maybe he was still trying to figure out where to put me. After all, it was a favor he was doing.

Dad shook his head. "I realize now that what you did wasn't a spur-of-the-moment thing where you were acting out or anything like that. I don't know what happened, but after seeing the doorbell camera video, I know he must've pushed you hard."

"He did." But I didn't want to go into that here.

"So, we're good. You don't have to work at the coffee shop unless you want to. I know you haven't started yet. You just had the meeting."

"It's your last summer," Papa told me. "Next summer, it will be all work… you can take this summer. Besides, if you want to work a little, you can come work for me. Or help Dad at his office."

Both of which would've paid better than the coffee place, guaranteed. "I'll think about it," I told them.

"With that settled…" Dad popped a french fry into his mouth. "What's the real story with you and Cobb?"

"We're friends." The answer was so automatic that it should've been received without question. My dads questioned everything.

"Then why do you have an edge of panic on your face because we're talking about him?"

Papa put a hand up like he was stopping me before I tried to play it off. "And don't try to tell us it isn't him when it's only there when we talk about him today. It hasn't been there any other time."

I took a deep breath. My dads and I could talk about everything. I hadn't told them about Owen as a choice but this wasn't going to be any different. "We had sex last night," I told him, not lowering my voice because we were in a restaurant. It wasn't like I was being loud and there wasn't anyone else in the booth behind him.

Dad's jaw tightened and he winced. "So you're together?"

I shook my head. "We're not. We just had sex. We're friends... who help each other out?" I shrugged because that might've been the dumbest sentence I'd ever uttered.

"Ah..." Papa nodded his head slowly like he knew what was going on. How could he when I didn't? "In our day, that was called 'friends with benefits.'"

I cringed. "Yeah, I don't like that and it was a one-time thing. No big deal."

Dad took a deep breath then leaned his folded arms on the table. "You sure it's not a big deal? We can talk about this."

"I don't need to." I pushed my plate away. I was done eating for sure. "It had been a long time and… It was just once. No need to go into it."

Dad said, "OK," then he leaned back, watching me the way he did when he was trying to figure out what I wasn't telling him. He wouldn't push, though.

We finished up, Dad paid, then we headed to the park. The seats were right by the home team's dugout, which was uncomfortable for me, to say the least. Great seats, though, and when I caught a glimpse of Cobb, he gave me the guy head nod. I waved a lame hand then focused on the game. At least he wasn't pitching.

He wouldn't be out there on the mound taunting me with every freaking movement.

Camden showed up right as the last inning ended. It was a win for Kalamazoo and I knew that next she'd take us down to wait for him by the clubhouse.

That's where Dad, Papa, Camden, and I were

when the players started filing out of the clubhouse. Man, they could change quickly. Camden waved her brothers over and introduced them to my dads. Brooks didn't hang around. After shaking my dads' hands, he said he had to go to the store.

"Where's Cobb?" Camden asked.

"He's coming," Urban told her. "He's got to deal with his future baby mama drama real quick."

Camden reached out and slapped Urban's arm as his gaze slid over to me. My dad's eye weighed heavily on me and everyone was looking at me as I stared at the wall behind him.

"You're an idiot," Silas said, then he pushed him away from us.

"Sorry about that," Camden said. "My brothers can be idiots."

"Not a big deal," I told her and gave her what I hoped was a smile.

Cobb had baby mama drama. Future, which meant the baby wasn't here yet, which meant that sometime in the last nine months, he'd gotten a woman pregnant and then broken up with her. What could the drama be? Was he refusing to take care of his portion of the responsibility? Was she insisting that they be together.

None of this should matter to me. We were friends. Nothing more.

It felt like forever with my dads gazes burning a hole through me, waiting for me to explain, but I couldn't. I didn't know what that meant. Finally, Cobb came out of the clubhouse with a tight jaw and angry eyes.

Once he'd gotten to us, Camden looked at him and said, "Can I talk to you for a second?"

But I shook my head. "It's fine, Camden. There's really no need." She opened her mouth, but I silently pled for her to let it go, so she did and told us she'd see us later.

"These are my dads," I told him. "John and Christopher. Dads, this is my friend, Cobb."

Cobb shook their hands, but my dads weren't all that nice. They were stranger-pleasant and not Dad-nice. Cobb's brows pinched together in evident confusion. The words they said were clipped and full of tension.

"Are you ready?" he asked me.

Now, I didn't want to ride with him or do whatever else he had planned, but if I said *no* and went home with my dads, they'd know that what I'd heard bothered me.

That was the last thing I wanted to deal with.

I gave him the best smile I could muster. "Ready."

"Honey." Dad grabbed my arm and gently pulled me away from Cobb. "Are you all right with all of this?"

"Yeah, of course." My voice sounded more sure than I felt. "We're not together, Dad. We scratched an itch. That's it."

"That's not like you."

I took a deep breath out of frustration. "Maybe it is now. I don't know, but he and I aren't together. We're friends. He can have ten baby mamas. It has no effect on me. We're friends."

Convincing them wasn't the issue. I was trying to convince myself.

Though I would've thought that as my friend, he would've told me about all of this.

Then I realized he hadn't told me because this situation had to be the exact reason why he'd always been clear that he could only be friends with me. Or anyone. Nothing more.

And I'd stupidly let myself fall for him, anyway.

CHAPTER 16
COBB

I was beginning to wonder if Monroe even wanted to be here with me.

We'd talked about this. Game, dinner, hang out. I'd drive her home. But she walked beside me with her spine so straight that I wondered if she'd hurt herself in some way.

The game had happened. We'd won. She seemed to be having a good time with her dads in the stands, but when I'd come out of the clubhouse, something in the air had been different.

Everyone else had left the room, but I'd had to call the lawyer back. He'd left a message asking me to tonight, no matter how late it was.

I didn't think that'd be a good sign, but he wanted me to know that his office had received the documentation showing the pregnancy and timeline that he'd requested of the lawyers in New York. He talked a little about what was going to happen from here and I was done.

It was an irritating call because anything to do with that situation pissed me off, but at least I'd get to spend some time with Monroe. After looking over at her in my car, I had to add a *maybe* to that. She was sitting straight up with her hands in her lap.

"Are you hungry for anything in particular?" I asked, hoping it'd start a conversation.

"No." And her fucking tone.

What the fuck had changed? I was acting normal. She'd been gone when I'd woken up this morning, which had irritated me, but I'd figured it was better to just get over it.

Mayb it was regret. Did having sex with her ruin my chance at having her in my life? It wasn't supposed to be now it sure seemed like it.

"OK." I sighed. "Want to make something at my place?"

She shook her head but kept her eyes on the road in front of us.

"What do you want to do, then?" I asked her.

Finally she looked over at me, but the fire in her

eyes was more anger than anything else. "I'm fine with just going home."

"Want to cook at your place?"

"Not really."

I sighed. This was not part of the plans for tonight, but if she was any other friend, I would've already dropped her off. So, I turned at the next street to get to her apartment. We didn't talk the rest of the way and when I pulled into her driveway, she had the car door open before I had brought the car to a full stop.

"Thanks for the ride." She smiled, but it wasn't real. Clearly, she was pissed about something.

"No problem."

She slammed the door harder than she needed to, leaving me to get dinner alone. Which I was fine with, but I would much rather have hung out with her for a while. Instead, I sent Brooks a text asking if he wanted to meet me.

He responded pretty quickly, telling me to come to his house. So that was where I went.

Brooks had bought this house not long after he'd been drafted. Since he'd gone right to the Knights, he'd known he'd be staying in Kalamazoo for his entire career unless something dramatic happened. So he'd bought this huge house, not like the one we'd grown up in, but big enough for him and quite a few kids if he decided to have them.

He pulled the front door open before I'd knocked. When I stepped in, the house smelled like he'd already started cooking.

"Something smells good," I said.

"It'll be done soon. Come help make salad."

I stepped in and chuckled. "You need help with that?"

"No," he called over his shoulder. Brooks was a good cook. Excellent, really. He enjoyed it. "But I figured it'd give you something to do until you decide to tell me why you wanted to get dinner tonight."

"Can't I want to hang out with my big brother?" I went over to the sink to wash my hands before chopping the vegetables.

"Of course you can. I'm actually pretty awesome, so that would make sense." He stirred something on the stove. "But you said you had plans with Monroe tonight and friends or not, there's zero chance you'd pass that up to hang out with me." He pushed the cutting board my way. "Start chopping."

I shook my head but did what he'd instructed.

It wasn't until after dinner—a delicious salmon and rice, but let's not forget the salad—that we were sitting on his couch drinking coffee and watching a sports show recap what had happened at the game we'd won that it came up again.

"So really, what happened to your plans?" he asked.

"I don't fucking know."

"How can you not know." He adjusted himself so that he was sitting facing me. "I get it that you're lying to yourself that you and her are just friends. It's what you need to do right now. Fine, but there's no chance you wouldn't be at her place right now if you could be."

"We're just friends," I told him, though some of the things we'd done the night before flashed through my mind. "Good friends." I decided to add that last part because I'd seen her naked. We had to be good friends.

"Yeah, yeah." He brushed his hand through the air as he said it.

"I don't know. Seriously. Everything was fine, but when I came out of the clubhouse, met her dads, something was different. She's pissed at something. I don't know what."

"Has to be you," he said. I was about to protest when he added, "Or something to do with you. So what'd you do?"

"Why would I have had to do something?" I asked. He cocked his head to the side and looked at me, making me sigh. "We had sex last night."

His loud laugh filled his house. "How bad was it for her to be literally *angry* about it?"

I lifted my middle finger at him. "It wasn't bad, asshole. It was good. Really fucking good. She was gone when I woke up this morning and I hadn't seen or talked to her all day, so I don't fucking know."

"You're an idiot. Don't you know you're supposed to talk to the woman the next day unless you don't want to see her again?"

I shook my head. Sure, he didn't get my relationship with Monroe and he didn't need to. "It's not like that."

Against my better judgement, I told Brooks everything that had happened the night before. Or really the last couple of days. Why I'd had her stay at my apartment. Her falling asleep, but then not being able to sleep because "I made her hormones crazy." The fact that we both insisted it wouldn't mean anything and we'd be friends after. Only friends.

"Maybe she doesn't want to be only friends," he said.

"I don't think so," I told him.

"And why can you only be friends?" Brooks took a long drink of his coffee, watching my every move as I attempted to answer.

"I can't bring someone else into the bullshit New York situation. I have to get that done first. She doesn't want anything, either, but I suspect it's because of that dickhead ex."

Brooks set his coffee cup on the table then sat back. "You're both idiots, then."

"You know..." I pushed to my feet and set my own mug down. "You can fuck off. If I want to be told I'm an idiot over and over, I'd hang out with Dad."

Brooks snorted. "I'm just saying. Neither of you are being honest with yourselves or each other. You've been all tied up over her since the beginning." Now he pushed to his feet and stomped over to me until he was invading my space. "If you ever fucking compare me to Dad again, you're going to land on the DL."

I snickered. That was one thing sure to piss any of us off. "I didn't mean to do that. I just meant that he tells us we're idiots whenever the topic of a woman comes up and you know it."

Brooks stepped back. "I do know it." He sighed

and put his hands on my shoulders. Brooks was just barely taller than me, but his shoulders were much wider. It was what made him an excellent catcher. There was a lot of target behind the plate when he was there. "Listen, if you wait for everything to be right or for your life to be settled and in order, you're going to lose that woman. Our lives are never settled. It fucking sucks to be the wife or girlfriend of a professional athlete. And I know you want Monroe. You shouldn't wait."

My stomach clenched and turned, making me a little nauseous at the idea of how he might answer the question I was about to ask. "If I tell her and she thinks I'm the asshole in this situation, she'll never talk to me again."

"Why would she think that?" He stepped back and let his arms fall to his side.

"Because it doesn't really put me in the best light. You know that's why we're trying to keep it out of the press. It makes me sound like a deadbeat dad."

Brooks shook his head. "You two haven't known each other long, but I'd be willing to bet she'd believe you." He went back around to his place on the couch. "At the very least, you should find out why she's mad. It might be a simple fix having nothing to do with your non-baby mama. Besides... If Silas can get over the fact that he felt like he killed Amity's brother and they can be together... I think you should be able to do that with Monroe."

"To stay friends."

He chuckled. "Sure. Whatever."

My big brother was right in that regard. What a fucking dumbass I'd been to drive away knowing that Monroe was angry.

I left Brooks's house and headed back to her apartment. Maybe she wouldn't be mad anymore, but I was about to find out.

I pressed the doorbell and waited. It had a camera on it, so she'd know it was me. But it wasn't her voice that came over speaker. "Can I help you?" That was one of her dads, but I couldn't remember which.

"Hi, Mr. Phillips. Is Monroe around?"

The silence I was met with was deafening and long. Until the door opened and that beautiful strawberry-blonde was in front of me in what had to be pajamas and bare feet.

"What's up?" she asked, crossing her arms under her breasts. She wasn't wearing a bra and her nipples pebbled in the night air.

"Can we talk?" I asked and I could see the *no* on her lips.

Imagine my surprise when she said, "Sure. Come in."

She led me through the walkway and into her apartment, where she shut and locked the door behind me as I kicked off my shoes.

"We alone?" I asked and she nodded. "But one of your dads—"

"He's in the house," she told me. "I was in the bathroom when the bell rang and as you know, they have access to the video feed."

"Right."

Once again, her posture was as straight as a broom. Normally, she had good posture, but it wasn't so… forced.

"Want a drink?" she asked.

"No thanks."

Monroe stopped on her way to the kitchen and turned to face me. Her fingers played with the hem of her shirt and her feet rubbed together. She was either nervous or uncomfortable. Maybe both.

"What's going on?" I asked her.

She wouldn't meet my eye when she said, "I don't know what you mean."

"Come on." I moved closer to her. "What

happened between last night and today? You were gone when I woke up."

"Did you want me to still be there?"

"Yeah." That answer only mildly surprised me. "I thought we'd get breakfast, but I'm not mad that you weren't. You can leave whenever you want to. I just wanted you to stay last night because you wouldn't let me follow you home to make sure you were all right."

She blew out a breath that caught her hair. "Right. I get that."

"So what the fuck happened between then and now?"

"Nothing." She moved to walk away, but I reached out and grabbed her wrist to stop her.

"It's not nothing. You're upset."

She snapped her teeth together and took a deep breath. "I should've just come home last night. I can handle myself even with him. I've been doing it for months."

My body tensed. "You shouldn't have to."

"I know," she said quietly. "It's getting better. He was drunk the other night, but I haven't heard from him since. It's fine. You don't have to take care of me."

A tightening gripped my chest. "I would take

care of any of my friends, Monroe."

"You say that, but are we even friends?"

I Yanked my hand away from her like she was suddenly the sun that I was trying to hold on to. "What's that supposed to mean? Of course we are."

"I don't think we are, Cobb," she said, causing me to swallow hard.

"Why the fuck would that be, Monroe?"

She closed her eyes and sighed. "Nothing." Then she opened her eyes slowly. "It's nothing. I'm upset about something that I have no right to be upset about. We're fine."

The small distance between us was too much, so I took a large step toward her. If this was about sex last night... that, I couldn't undo. But I sure as fucking hell wanted to figure it out because at this point, I wanted Monroe in my life any way that I could have her.

Maybe one day both of us would be able to get our fucking lives in order and I could have her the way I desperately wanted to. Hell, at this point, I was almost willing to bring her into the shitstorm I was dealing with, even if I shouldn't.

It was selfish, but I guess I was a selfish bastard.

"What're you upset about?"

She looked away from me. "Nothing."

Using my index finger, I turned her head back toward me. "It's not nothing. I'd like to know," I told her much more gently than we had been speaking to each other. "I'll fix it if I can."

Our eyes locked as she warred with herself on whether to tell me or not, which already told me that it was about me or having to do with me. Thinking back to everything since I'd come off the road trip, nothing came to mind.

So I waited.

Finally, she sighed again and wrapped her arms under her breasts.

"I found out today that you have a baby mama and I don't know…" She shrugged and squeezed her arms tighter as my world tilted on its axis and my stomach dropped. It felt like I'd been punched in the chest. "It bothered me. Even though I know there's no reason for it to. We're not together, but I thought… as a friend, that would've been something you'd tell me."

And now I fucking needed to.

CHAPTER 17
MONROE

*C*obb looked like someone had punched him in the stomach. He took a step back as if I'd slapped him and his face flushed in what I thought was anger.

I should've kept my mouth shut.

He closed his eyes and hadn't opened them back up yet. Clearly, he hadn't intended for me to find out at all.

"You should just go, Cobb. I'll talk to you tomorrow." My plan was to get over this before then. Why had I let what Urban had said bother me so much?

Would I have been angry if Asher or Reana had a baby daddy? I mean, yeah. If they didn't tell me about it, I would have been.

As I sat there lying to myself that this was exactly the same thing, Cobb shook his head. "How did you even find out about that?"

Sure. That was what he'd want to know. "It doesn't matter. Like I said, there's no reason for me to be upset about this. You're not my boyfriend. We're not together. We're not a couple. What you do is your business and you're not required to tell me anything."

With his hands on his hips, he sighed. "You're right. We're not any of those things because neither of us can be. We both said friends only, Monroe."

"I know," I snapped, then I swallowed hard. "I did say it wasn't rational, right? I'll get over it. It was just a surprise."

"I didn't tell you because of how it would sound. You'd have run the other direction and I really didn't want that."

I held up my hand to stop him. "It's fine, Cobb. I said it's fine. Just take that and go. I'll be much friendlier tomorrow."

"Wait," he said, as if he something had just snapped in his head. "Are you upset that I didn't tell you or that you think I have a baby mama?"

My stomach sank. This was why I wanted him to leave so he wouldn't ask questions. "Both. OK? It doesn't make sense to me, either, but here we are." I stomped past him into the kitchen to pull a bottle of water out of the fridge then took the longest drink of my life. My hands vibrated against the cold. "Can we be done? I'm not proud of myself today. I'd like to sulk in peace."

"Do you want to be together?" he asked, making me stumble two steps back as if his words had a physical weight that pushed me.

"What? No. We said friends only."

He shook his head as he closed the distance between us, causing me to take yet another step away.

"Monroe," he said quietly. "Are you sure about that? Are you sure you don't want to be with me?"

My stomach felt suddenly empty as my mouth dried right up. "Fine. I guess I can't deny it because I let my feelings get the best of me today. After last night... it felt different. *I've* felt different and it hasn't mattered how much I've been trying to deny it even to myself. I think I've been developing *more than friend* feelings for a while."

The corners of his mouth tipped up like he was about to smile.

"Don't worry," I told him. "I'll get vaccinated against feelings tomorrow. I'll be fine tomorrow."

Cobb took the two steps toward me and placed a hand on each side of my neck, a thumb stroking each cheek.

"If you want more than friends, Monroe, I'm happy to give that to you. I wanted you the moment I heard you give that guy hell in the coffee shop. There are some things in my life—one thing—that I wanted to get cleared up beforehand, but I wouldn't have been able to deny you. You said you only wanted to be friends and I wasn't going to fuck that up."

Leaning into his touch, I snorted. "I wanted the ex-dickhead to go away. I didn't want anyone else— you—getting caught up in that. I didn't want anyone to fight my battles for me."

He leaned down so that we were at the same height. "I'll fight every one of your battles for you, Monroe. But only if you want me to."

"I didn't want to lose you in my life," I said quietly. "But if you have a baby coming—"

"I don't," he told me. When I was about to protest, he added, "I don't and I'll explain it all, but right now, I really need to kiss you."

My entire body liquified at his words and he didn't wait for me to say *yes*. I didn't need to. He probably saw everything plainly on my face.

Cobb's lips met mine, gently at first as he wrapped an arm around my waist to pull me to him. The other hand pushed into my hair, tightening at the base. I slid my hands up to his shoulders and dug my fingernails in.

The shockwave of his groan against my mouth reached my toes. He pushed his tongue into my mouth. His hands slid down my legs and lifted so that I could wrap them around his waist. Then he moved us through my apartment. I didn't care where we went right now. All I cared about was him.

It wasn't until he'd dropped me on my bed that I knew he'd taken us into my bedroom. I was so focused on Cobb surrounding me, soaking him up with all of my senses, that it wouldn't have mattered.

He reached back and pulled his shirt over his head, exposing all of that beautiful, golden skin. Looking up at him through my lashes, I found his heated gaze on me.

With trembling hands, I slowly undid his jeans and pushed them down his legs. He kicked them away once I couldn't reach anymore. Then I hooked my thumbs in his boxer briefs and slid those down, releasing his erection. His cock bounced out, but he caught it in his hand and pumped it once as it glistened at the tip.

I licked my lips before replacing his hand with my own. The muscles in his stomach tightened and he groaned at my touch. Gently, I stroked him up and then down three times before pushing his cock past my lips. A move that caused him to fist my hair tightly, though he didn't try to control my movements.

Instead, I got to enjoy the taste of him, the way that I was making him lose control. And I couldn't believe that I'd been insisting to myself that I didn't want this. Didn't want him.

So fucked up.

At least we were here now.

I continued to bob my head over him, taking him deeper with each pass until he hit the back of my throat. Then he stepped back, sounding out of breath.

I looked up and ran my thumb over my bottom lip, making his jaw tense and causing him to shake his head slowly.

"It's not ending there," he said.

He smoothly yanked my shirt over my head. My nipples pebbled in the air conditioning. I'd been in my pajamas and no sane woman wore a bra to bed if they didn't have to and I didn't. Then he did the same to my shorts, taking my panties with it and tossing them both behind him.

Cobb wrapped a large hand around each thigh and pulled as he dropped to his knees. He pushed my legs apart and buried his head between them. The first touch of his tongue nearly sent me to the moon. Everything Cobb did was perfect, like he already knew exactly what I wanted. Sure, we'd been together last night, but that had been a means to an end for both of us. An itch that had needed to be scratched.

This felt... different.

His magic fingers teased me as his hot mouth sucked the skin on my thigh before sealing over my clit. It didn't take long for the pressure to build. I threaded my fingers into his hair and pulled him against me. That pressure burst into a million stars as I floated on a cloud.

I'd had orgasms before, but this... I couldn't put into words.

Once the initial waves had subsided, Cobb pulled back and wiped a hand over his mouth.

"Please tell me you have—"

"Condoms. Drawer." I pointed at the night-stand drawer. I hadn't needed them in about a year, but I'd bought some when I'd first been going to go out with the ex-asshole in case I'd needed them. Clearly, I never had, but the date was still good on them.

He tore the drawer open like a crazy man, ripping the box apart instead of opening it on the end. He tore open the condom and slid it over him. I watched as my legs trembled.

Then he was hovering over me, kissing me and stroking me before leaning back and watching himself sink inside me. I groaned and he rested his forehead against mine.

"One second." His eyes were squeezed shut.

He was about to lose it right then and there. Because of me. My chest swelled. This man was wanted by many, could've had anyone he wanted, probably—there were groupies for everything—but he was here with me, almost cumming after one stroke.

I didn't have a confidence deficiency, but knowing that I could do this to him... had my ego swelling.

Finally, he started to move.

Everything he did set me on fire. Making him lose control might've boosted my ego, but the way he played me like a violin should've boosted his. It'd never been like this for me. Not once.

I even pouted when he pulled out. At least until he told me to roll over. I thought I'd get on all fours, but that wasn't what Cobb wanted. Instead, I lay down on my stomach with my hands beside my head. He pulled my hips up to push into me then flattened them to the mattress, spreading my legs as far apart as they would go. His chest was against my back and his arms created a cage around my head.

Cobb was everywhere, pushing me toward another orgasm. Then he lifted one of my legs out beside me, creating yet another angle, and that was all it took. I fell off that cliff again, not caring if I ever hit the ground.

But at least he was right there with me.

Slowly, he pulled out of me and set my leg right again. When I didn't move at first, he said, "You all right?"

"Perfect," I mumbled into the mattress as I gave him a thumbs-up.

He snickered then said he'd be right back. Had to take care of the condom. I lay there, basking in the best sex of my entire life, until he came back. Then I knew I had to go clean myself up before I could cuddle into him and stretch all the muscles he'd just used that I'd forgotten I had.

Once I finished, we were lying in my bed, silent, me with my head against his bare chest and him lightly trailing his fingertips up and down my arm. We still had a bunch to talk about, I supposed, but right here with him like this was absolute perfection.

"Did you say you were going to get vaccinated against me?" he asked, that low voice slicing through the quiet afterglow.

I snickered and buried my face into his chest. "No," I said once I'd lifted my face again. "I said I was going to get vaccinated against feelings."

He chuckled quietly in his chest. "I guess that makes it better."

I reached up, using one hand to hold him in place, and kissed the spot right below his jawbone. It was the farthest up I could reach, then I snuggled down beside him again.

"It does make it better," I explained. "It wasn't you I was trying to guard against. It was all feelings."

"And now?"

"I'm not sure a vaccine would work. I was guarding myself because you didn't want a relationship. You couldn't be mine. It was to protect myself."

"I was yours the minute you stepped up to the table in the coffee shop."

Biting my lips together was the only way to keep the squeal I wanted to release from embarrassing me.

"Well, I know that now…"

Cobb squeezed me to him and kissed the top of my head. "Do you want to talk about the other stuff now? Or tomorrow?"

I sighed. It was only a matter of time before we had to extricate ourselves from this cozy bed we'd created for ourselves. I pushed off him and swung my legs over the side of the bed, got my panties over my feet so that I could put them on as I stood up, then grabbed his T-shirt and dropped that over me.

"If we're going to do that, I want to be eating ice cream." Then I hurried out of the room.

Moments later, I had a pint of Mackinac Island Fudge on the counter with two spoons and Cobb came out of the bedroom in just his boxer briefs. I could see the outline of everything and this time, I looked without shame.

The man had been built by the gods. Or maybe

he'd been built by baseball because every inch of him was hard muscle. Not large, but lean, almost like a swimmer. He was so damn tall.

"You're sharing?" He raised an eyebrow.

"I thought it only fair."

I'd taken a seat on one of the white barstools at the kitchen island. Luckily, I could fold my legs beneath me. There were some benefits to being short. Cobb definitely couldn't. He was too big. I used to think my apartment was perfect and for me, it was. But I could see how it could be a problem if there was a second person living here. Not that I was thinking Cobb would live here. That'd be ridiculous.

Aside from the fact that we hadn't known each other long, I wouldn't bring a guy to live basically in my dads' house.

We each took a couple of bites in silence, but I knew it wouldn't last.

"Do you just want me to tell you or do you want to ask questions first?" he asked, leaving it up to me.

Right now... I honestly didn't want to think about it.

"Would you mind if we waited until tomor-row?" I asked. "I know I was so upset earlier, but this clearly isn't your first time with a woman. We change our minds sometimes."

"Are you sure?"

I nodded. "Earlier, you telling me was all I wanted because I was so pissed that you hadn't. I still maintain that I had no right to be upset. But I think it was just compounded because..." I blew out a breath. "This morning, I didn't hear from you. At the game, you gave me the head nod but didn't even look that happy to see me. I don't know." I shrugged, trying to work up the courage to say what needed to be said. "It felt like you went back to just friends so easily. That I was crazy for thinking there could be more."

"But now you know that you aren't crazy, right?"

I snickered. "I know I'm not crazy for that reason, anyway. The reason I want to wait until tomorrow is because if we're starting something here, I don't want it to be marred with anything else. I just want it to be us." My gaze met his hard-to-read dark eyes. "*If* we're starting something here."

"Oh, we're starting something. Actually, we're continuing something since I think this whole time has been foreplay, anyway."

"What?" I asked with humor in my voice.

"It has been. Since the moment I met you. We're definitely doing something here. I already told you that I'm yours."

I blew out a slow breath. "Then tomorrow. All of our skeletons can come out of the closet tomorrow."

He agreed and we went back to eating our ice cream. Until he said, "You've got some on your chin." Then he leaned over and licked it off my chin quicker than I could raise my hand.

That lick turned into a kiss, which turned into our spoons being dropped on the counter and Cobb pushing the ice cream away. He lifted me then set me down roughly on the counter, cupped my cheeks, and kept his soft lips on mine. That kiss didn't end until he was lifting his T-shirt over my head. Then he leaned back to look.

Cobb ran his tongue over his bottom lip then grabbed one of the spoons we'd dropped. The ice cream was melty and he held it over me, letting the creamy goodness drip onto my chest, down between my breasts to my stomach. It probably would've kept going, but he leaned down and licked it off my stomach, then trailed his tongue up between my breasts then to my chest.

A cold, thrilling chill crawled over my body.

Then Cobb took a bite of the ice cream, smiled, and took a nipple into his mouth. The cold of the ice cream turned his normally warm mouth into an iceberg, causing me to yelp in surprise. My nipple hardened before he scraped his teeth over it.

"Cobb." I gasped and pulled at him, but there was nothing to hold on to. His golden skin was on display, which meant no shirt to pull. "Cobb." I sounded needy, even to my ears.

"I'm working on it," he told me, then he took the other nipple into his mouth.

"I need you," I said, hoping that he'd get what I meant so I wouldn't have to say it.

I needed him inside me. The yearning was too much for me to wait. He swiftly tore my panties down my legs then pushed all the way into me in one movement, making me catch my breath and come undone all at the same time.

He hit exactly the right spot. The waves crashed over me as he didn't hesitate to pump himself in and out of me at a pace that I could never keep up with.

Soon after, he made a sound in his throat, his movements less precise and he slowed himself to a stop, dropping his head to my shoulder.

The sound of us each catching our breaths filled the air of my kitchen.

"Sorry that was a quick one," he said, sounding as out of breath as I felt.

My eyes were closed as I clung to his shoulders. "It was perfect," I told him. "I came as soon as you pushed into me." Then I opened my eyes to find him watching me. "You make me needy."

He chuckled then watched as he pulled himself out of me. "I've been accused of worse things." As if he'd said something horrible, he winced. It had to do with baby mama drama. I somehow knew it.

"Let's get some sleep." I lightly tapped his shoulder. "But I'm not sure I can walk." My legs were still slightly vibrating from the orgasm he'd just given me. Or maybe it was the number in the last twenty-four hours.

Cobb chuckled, then swept me up into his arms and took me to bed. I still had to use the bathroom, but I enjoyed the ride anyway.

After we'd each cleaned up again, I was tucked under his arm, half-asleep when he said, "I got carried away."

"Me too," I said because I knew exactly what he was talking about. Lightly tapping his chest, I continued. "It'll be fine. I'm on birth control if that's what you're worried about."

He didn't respond one way or another to that subject. "I always use a condom, Monroe. I wouldn't put you at risk."

The biggest, most tired smile I could muster curved my lips. "I know, baby. I know."

Did I know? Not really, but he was sincere and right now, all I wanted was the beautiful exhaustion that came from what we'd been doing tonight.

It was the best way to block out the reality of what was coming tomorrow.

CHAPTER 18
COBB

*M*onroe's body was still pressed into my side when I opened my eyes the next morning. I ran a hand over her hip then squeezed her to me. Last time, she'd bolted sometime before I'd gotten up, so having her here with me was new. Then again, we were in her apartment. Where the hell would she go?

Suddenly, that warm body next to me moved, sliding her bare leg against mine and wrapping her arm around my stomach.

"Good morning," her sleepy voice said as she looked up at me.

"Morning." I leaned down and kissed the top of her head.

Before either of us could say anything else,

someone or something started to knock. Monroe furrowed her brows while I went on high alert.

The outside door was too far for anyone to be knocking on and us hear it. This was on the inside door.

"It must be one of my dads." She pushed the blanket off her. She was wearing my T-shirt as she hurried to the door. "Hey," she answered.

As soon as she'd hurried out, I began to get dressed. If her dads were going to be in here, I shouldn't be wearing only my boxer briefs. Even if they were aware that she had a sex life, they probably didn't want to see it.

"Just wanted to check on you before I leave for work," her dad said. I tried to remember which one's voice that was, but I'd met them so briefly after the game that it was impossible.

"I'm fine, Papa." That would be Chris, as he'd been introduced to me yesterday.

"You sure?"

"I'm sure."

"Want me to stay and talk about it? I don't have to go right in."

"No." That was when I went out to the living room without a shirt on. Hey, she still had it on and I wasn't about to hide in the bedroom like I was sixteen years old. Monroe glanced back at me then to her dad again. "We can talk later."

Chris eyed me and the message was received. *Don't fuck my daughter over.* It was good he sent the message, especially since I didn't plan to.

"We *will* talk later," he responded.

Then she shut the door.

"Sorry about that." She played with the hem of my shirt.

"Not a problem," I told her. "At least they care about you, but it seems like they take a step back to let you run your life."

"They do." She slowly walked toward me. "For the most part. I still get a lecture here or there, but otherwise, it's good. They don't interfere unless they think I'm going to get hurt."

I ran my tongue over my bottom lip. "So you'll be having a conversation with them later." She nodded. Of course she would be. After all, they probably knew about my situation now.

"Can I use your toothbrush?" I asked her because before I'd kiss her the way I wanted to, I'd brush the morning breath away.

She scrunched her face in disgust. "No. That's disgusting."

I chuckled. "You had my dick in your mouth

last night and my face in your pussy, but you won't let me use your toothbrush?"

Her cheeks flamed. "That's different. I have extras under the sink."

With another laugh, I went to the bathroom to brush my damn teeth. Instead of throwing the toothbrush away, I put it next to hers on the shelf. Chances were, I'd need it again.

When I came out, Monroe was in the pajamas she'd been wearing last night when I'd gotten here and my T-shirt was folded neatly and sitting on the corner of the island. I'd put it on, but not yet because from what I could see, Monroe thoroughly appreciated me not wearing it.

"So…" She drew the word out as she handed me a cup of coffee. Sugar, creamer, and a flavored creamer were sitting on the counter between us.

"Come here," I told her as I patted the stool beside me. Once she'd climbed up, I was reminded of what had happened the last time we'd been sitting here. No time for that today. She was careful not to touch the countertop, which made me laugh. "I came out after you went to sleep and cleaned it. Won't be sticky."

Then she set her arm on it and her cup down.

"Well… ice cream did kind of get everywhere and we didn't even put it away."

"I did," I told her. "Well, I threw it away because it was pretty melted."

She pushed her bottom lip out. "Such a waste of good ice cream."

"We'll get more," I promised. "And you'll never be able to convince me that it was a waste."

For the second time that morning, her cheeks blushed.

"Now," I continued, "you want to know about my baby mama drama."

Her face grew more serious. Gone was the small smile that had appeared when I'd told her she would never convince me that the way we'd used the ice cream last night had been a waste. She'd been remembering just like I had been.

"You don't have to tell me." But she was looking into her coffee and not at me. "I shouldn't have let it upset me."

"No. You should have." I gently pulled her chin so she'd have to turn in her seat and face me. "I should've told you. I just thought it'd make me sound fucking awful. But I didn't lie when I told you that I don't have any baby mama drama. Not really."

"But your brother said—"

A flame ignited in my chest, hot and immediately angry. "Which brother?" Even to me, that tone sounded dangerous. I wasn't going to literally kill my brother, but other than that, I could imagine maiming him right now. I just needed to know which one to imagine.

"It doesn't matter." She averted her eyes again.

"Monroe, it matters to me. One of my brothers talked out of turn and I'd like to know which one."

She sighed and bit her lips together before saying, "Urban, but I think he thought I knew. He wasn't, like, tattling on you. When Camden asked where you were he said you had baby mama drama to take care of. I think he was just comfortable."

"Yeah." *Fucking Urban.* "Too fucking comfortable. I get why he said it, but… never mind. You don't need to worry about it. I'll talk to him later.

"Was he lying?" Her blue eyes looked hopeful as she looked up at me.

I grabbed each side of the stool and yanked to bring her closer to me. She was between my legs as close as she could get when I set my hands on the tops of her thighs and rubbed.

"He wasn't lying, exactly," I explained. "It's just not fully accurate." I blew out a breath as she waited. "I met this woman, the daughter of the New York team's owner." She bit her lips together and waited. "Anyway, she wanted to hook up, I didn't. I was gentle and honestly, I didn't know she was the owner's daughter. Anyway, a month later, she says she's pregnant with my kid. There's no possibility because I never touched her. But it pissed her dad off."

"I bet. Was that how you ended up here?"

I nodded. "He didn't want me there anymore because he thought I'd knocked his daughter up and wasn't living up to my end of the deal." I sighed. "If the press hears about this, it won't be pretty for me. Plenty of professional athletes have baby mamas they don't acknowledge. I wouldn't do that, but they don't know. Anyway, it's bad press for the team, for my family… for you."

Her eyes widened and she sat up straight. "Me? Why me?"

After tucking a piece of hair behind her ear, I said, "If you're with me, it will affect you. You'll have to hear about it and see it. We don't necessarily get paparazzi following us, but it'll be in every interview I do and it'll be a non-stop headache. It'll look like I cheated on you. Your friends and dads will asked you about it. I could go on."

She furrowed her brows, "But I didn't know you then."

"They won't care. So far, she's proven she is actually pregnant and the timeline is right for that kid to be mine, but until I had sex with you, it'd been months. I didn't touch her."

Monroe cupped my cheek then ran her hand down the side of my neck until it reached my shoulder. "I believe you."

"You do?"

She shrugged. "Yeah. Why would you lie? It's not like I even knew you then." She wet her lips quickly. "I do wish you'd told me before your brother blabbed it to me, but you didn't owe me that."

"Yes, I did."

"We were friends."

I narrowed my eyes together and cocked my head to the side. "Do you honestly think we were ever just friends?" She took a breath and parted her lips. "Brooks told me that I was fucked the day you danced in the rain at my parents' house."

"He did?" Her grin was wide.

I nodded. "Sure did. We were only fooling ourselves and no one else."

Monroe bit into her bottom lip, which had me

far too focused on her mouth. "I guess that's probably true." Our gazes met and held for several seconds before Monroe looked away shyly. *Shy* wasn't a word I ever would've used to describe her before now. "Do you want breakfast?"

That was when I had to pull back. "Yes, but I should probably go." She pushed her bottom lip out to pout, so I leaned over and pulled it between my teeth. "I have to shower and do a few things before getting to the park."

"Fine." She had the tone of being fake angry or put out or something, but the curve of her lips told me she wasn't serious.

"Come to the game tonight," I told her. "I'll have a ticket at will call. You'll have to sit with Camden and Amity, most likely."

"That's fine." She swung her legs around then hopped off the stool. "I should probably shower first, too. I'm all sticky." I snorted and she rolled her eyes. "From the ice cream."

"Oh, I know."

I cupped her face between my large hands and leaned down to kiss her. The longer my mouth worked against hers, the more I wanted to walk her right back into her bedroom. But there wasn't time.

Damn it.

"I'll see you later," she whispered breathlessly once I'd finally brought our kiss to an end.

"Yes, you will."

I put my shirt back on and pushed my feet into my shoes. After kissing her two more times, I forced myself to leave her apartment.

Didn't stop me from thinking about her the rest of the day.

That is, until I found Urban at the ballpark. He was walking in the same time as me.

"What the fuck were you thinking?" I asked him. We each had a bag over our shoulders as we did every day that we came here.

"What are you talking about?"

Urban and I were about the same height. He was a bit bulkier than I was, muscle wise, but not much. And all of my brothers and I looked alike. Sure, we styled our hair differently, but it was the same color, as were our eyes.

"Yesterday after the game? 'Baby mama drama'? Are you fucking serious?"

He cringed before entering the park. "Yeah, sorry about that."

"'Sorry about that'?" I asked. "That's it?"

He stopped and turned to me. "I don't really know what else you want me to say. How the fuck was I supposed to know that Monroe didn't know about that? You two have been inseparable since you met. I know you're '*just friends*'"—the fucker used air quotes on that—"but I assumed you'd told her. I'm sorry."

"Her dads were there," I countered as I folded my arms over my chest. "Did you think about that?"

"Not really." At least he was honest. "It just came out and I am sorry about that. If it makes you feel better, Camden did hit me."

I snorted then got walking again. "It does make me feel better."

"Is Monroe pissed?"

"She was. I made sure she wasn't anymore."

His laughter echoed down the hall. "Fucking finally. You fucked her into not being mad at you? That's a skill, man."

I shook my head at him. "That's not what I meant. I explained it to her this morning. She's not mad."

He stopped walking again. "You're telling me you didn't fuck her?"

Anger boiled in my stomach. I didn't like him talking about her like that. "Fuck off. Would you like me talking about Everly like that? Urban, did you fuck her yesterday? Do you fuck her out of being mad at you? That's bullshit."

He shrugged and started walking. "You have a point, but yeah, I did and yes, I do."

I'd arrived here today irritated at my brother. Now, we were both laughing like fucking fifteen-year-olds.

During the down time before the game... before all the shit got put away thirty minutes before the start, I called the lawyer back. He'd called when I'd been throwing my bullpen session and if I waited, I wouldn't be able to talk to him today.

"I want this to be over," I told him once the greetings were out of the way. "I don't want me or anyone else to have to deal with this. What can I do?" Mostly, I didn't want anything ugly touching Monroe.

"I know you do. You just have to be patient."

I liked this guy, but fuck, was this moving slowly.

"What the fuck does she want from me? Other than saying that kid is mine?"

He sighed and went silent for too long. Clearly, I wasn't going to like this. "She did ask for a face-to-face meeting with you. I rejected it because it didn't seem like something you'd want to do."

"I don't want to see her."

"Right. I knew that. That does seem to be a sticking point for her. She says she won't consider the paternity test without seeing you first. And actually, I got a call from her lawyer yesterday that she's setting up some interviews."

"Fuck." I pulled the phone away from my ear and fought everything inside me telling me to throw it. "So she's going to ruin my reputation? Or try to? Why? I don't even know her. She doesn't know me. Yet everyone's going to believe her."

"They usually do," he said and at least he was being nice about it. "Now, I did find out, through less official channels, that you seem to be the first player to turn her down."

"What?"

"She's a bit of a cleat chaser. Isn't that what they're called?"

I sighed. "Yeah."

"Anyway, you said *no*. She's angry about that. But she's unwilling to have any further conversation until she meets with you. We'll have to wait it out at least another few weeks so that she's far enough along to do a paternity test. Now, she isn't asking for anything, so it's going to be hard to compel, but we'll work on it."

Fuck this woman. I was the first to turn her

down? That couldn't be right. But why would that trigger this?

Talk about not understanding women...

"Let me talk to my girl," I told him. "I don't want to do anything that will make her uncomfortable. If she's cool with it, I'll meet her."

"I do think that will move this along. She's used to getting her way." He was clearly talking about Hannah. "Letting her win a little might make her feel like she's in control again and she'll drop this."

"Yeah. I'll let you know."

"You can text me anytime tonight," he said. "She's willing to fly in next day, so we could get this done tomorrow if you decide to."

Now that was appealing. Having this behind me so I could focus on Monroe was exactly what I wanted.

She was at the game sitting with my sister and Urban's woman. Thankfully, my sister had given her the pass that she could wear around her neck to get down to the clubhouse after the game. I'd made sure that had been taken care of after my conversation with Urban this afternoon.

Monroe was waiting for me after the game. I slipped my hand in hers and walked away from everyone.

"Your place or mine tonight?" I asked, though realistically, we weren't going to be spending every night together.

"Actually, I'm going to Papa's shop early tomorrow morning, so you might want to stay home alone."

"Never."

She snorted. "No, really. I can't keep interrupting your schedule, right?"

"What are you going in for?"

"He wants to show me this piece he just made. He tried something new and it worked, so he wants to show it off. Dad's going too. Took some time off in the morning. But I can see you after. Like for lunch."

I brought us to a stop before we left the building. After quickly glancing around, I saw a room that no one was likely in and slipped in there with her.

"I talked to my lawyer today," I told her, then I explained the entire conversation. Including the fact that Hannah wanted a face-to-face meeting. "I won't do it if it makes you uncomfortable."

She furrowed her brows. "Why would I be uncomfortable?"

I shrugged. "I'd be meeting a woman who says

she's pregnant with my kid. I'm not sure how it will go."

Monroe gave me a sweet smile. "I'm not worried, Cobb. You should know that I don't do jealous. I don't worry about people cheating on me. If someone's going to cheat on me, then they're going to cheat. Me worrying about it won't change that, so why bother?"

I grabbed her with a hand on each hip and pulled her toward me. "I'd never cheat on you."

"I didn't think you would because I don't worry about it. Just know that if you ever did, there are no second chances when it comes to that."

"I won't need a second chance."

"Then what's there to worry about?" she asked. That, I didn't have an answer to. "You should do it, though. Figure out why she's pinning this on you. Want me to come with you?"

Oh, I didn't know if that was a good idea and Monroe must've seen it because she snickered.

"I didn't mean into the actual meeting. I could wait out in the hall or somewhere else. Just for moral support."

I sighed. "Fine. I'll take the meeting. The lawyer said she'd come in tomorrow."

"Must be nice to be able to afford last-minute

travel plans like that," she said. Though I was fairly certain her dads would've been able to without an issue.

"What's to afford? Daddy has a private plane."

"Ah. Yes. That does make it easier."

I kissed the top of her head and pulled her into my arms. "And yes, come with me. I don't want to be alone with her, so maybe we can leave the door open or something. Just knowing you're there will be perfect."

CHAPTER 19
COBB

*T*he last fucking thing I wanted to do today before the game was meet with the woman trying to control or ruin my life.

Could she actually ruin it? No, probably not. Could she control it? I wouldn't let her.

Monroe knew about all of this, so she wouldn't be taken by surprise and honestly, she'd taken the news pretty well.

Fuck, she believed me, which I hadn't thought anyone would do.

But could Hannah cause me a PR nightmare? Yeah, she fucking could.

Half an hour before we were supposed to meet —alone—I was waiting at the coffee shop where I'd met Monroe. That was the plan. Then she'd walk over with me to my lawyer's office, where the meeting was supposed to take place.

Hannah had offered to come to my apartment, but as far as I knew, she didn't have my address and I wasn't going to be the one to change that.

After ten minutes—no Monroe. I kept checking my phone and after five more minutes, I called her. Time was running out. My lawyer wanted to talk to me before the meeting and wanted me there twenty minutes early so that there'd be no chance of running into her on the way.

This conversation was supposed to be in a controlled environment. Manning wouldn't be part of it, watching it, and wasn't allowed to record it, so anything that happened would be my word against hers.

But the hope was that by meeting her, she'd admit she was lying and let me off the hook.

Finally, I couldn't wait anymore. Monroe didn't answer her phone and she wasn't here like she'd said she'd be, which left me with a lot of worry. First, that something had happened to her on the way here, or second, had the reality of all this set in and she'd changed her mind?

Fuck, I hoped not.

Still, I hurried over to my lawyer's office next door.

I was sitting in a conference room—alone, waiting for Hannah to show up.

Which she did two minutes after our meeting time.

She was wearing a sundress and holding a stomach that wasn't there like she was trying to show off that she was pregnant, but it was so early that there was nothing to show off. Her brown hair was in loose braids with wisps of hair around her face.

Hannah was an attractive woman who could probably get any guy she wanted. Other than me, anyway, which was part of the reason this didn't make sense. Manning said they'd verified that she was pregnant, so she wasn't faking it, which meant *someone* had gotten her that way.

Why wasn't she satisfied with going after *him*?

"Hi, Cobb," she said almost shyly once the receptionist had shut the door behind her. The room wasn't overly large, with a rectangle table in the middle that only sat, like, eight people. But the wall shared with the rest of the office was all glass. People would be able to see our interaction if not hear it.

Which I thought was by design. Witnesses who could say whether or not I touched her because given her crazy accusations, I didn't trust that she wouldn't make something else up.

"Hello." Then I waited on the other side of the table for her to speak. When she didn't, I said, "You're the one who wanted this meeting. You're going to have to start."

She wet her lips and looked away shyly. This was an act. I knew that much about her. She'd been forward as hell at that party.

"I thought that by us being face to face, we could talk a little. You'd get to know me better and see how good we could be together."

I snorted. "What?"

That was probably the wrong reaction because her eyes narrowed. "We could be. I know everything about you."

"False," I told her immediately. "You know everything that's on Wikipedia or whatever. You don't know me. We met for, like, ninety seconds weeks ago. That's not knowing me."

"Exactly." She took a step forward and rested her hands on the back of a chair. I wasn't about to sit down because no matter what, I'd make sure she was on the other side of this table from me. "This is our chance to get to know each other."

"You're kidding, right?"

Her face hardened. Nope. Not kidding. There was something off-putting in the way she was talking to me.

Hannah would've been used to being around baseball players. She would've grown up with it. So why was she being like this with me?

"Well, it's enough to know that we'd be good together and from everything I've read, you'd be a great father. So why not just accept this?"

"Are you insane?" I snapped. Her mouth dropped open and I cringed. I shouldn't have said that. The last thing I wanted to do was rile her up more than I had to. "I'm sorry I said that, but what about the actual father of your baby? Shouldn't he have the chance to know his kid?"

She rolled her eyes at me. "*You're* the father of my baby."

"But I'm not." I said it louder than I needed to and threw my hands in the air in frustration. Anger turned my stomach, but I'd have to keep that under wraps to not make this whole thing worse. "I'm not, Hannah, and you know it. As soon as there's a paternity test, everyone will know it."

"I won't do the test," she said right away.

"The courts can force you to, but can you explain to me why you're doing this?"

"I want to be with you. I think that's obvious." She started to pace but then turned quickly to come to my side of the table. I stepped back, making sure she wasn't within arm's reach. "All of my research says you're a good guy." Fucking research? "You come from money. You make a ton of money. You'd be able to take care of us and you come from a baseball dynasty. Everyone knows your family."

I furrowed my brows. "Money? You dad has a shit ton of it. I don't really think you need to worry."

"You don't understand." She shook her head. "My dad will disown me if I don't get you to take responsibility."

"Why is that?"

"Because I told him you're the father." She took a deep breath then dropped the axe. "I could ruin your career," she said, sounding mildly threatening. "I could. I could go to the press and tell them that you got me pregnant—maybe it wasn't totally consensual—and now you're shirking your responsi-bility. No team is going to want to touch you."

She wasn't wrong in general. If she made allegations of it not being totally consensual, most teams wouldn't want to touch me with a ten-foot pole until it was figured out in court. But she forgot that my grandpa owns the team I was currently on and my mother managed it.

"You could try," I told her. "But I'd bet that I'd stay right here in Kalamazoo without much issue." I sighed. "Look, I only took this meeting to convince you to stop whatever this is against me. It's a lie and we both know it. I didn't touch you at that party."

She shrugged. "We were talking closely. Other people probably thought something was going on."

"They can think whatever they want." That wasn't my problem. "But you know that I didn't take you up on your offer."

She shrugged once more. "Maybe I don't take rejection well." She took a slow step forward.

Again, I snorted. "I think that's an understatement."

She narrowed her eyes on me. "Maybe I'm a little spoiled. I tend to get what I want and my mother told me that if you are what I want, I should go after you. Do what it takes to make you mine. That's all I'm doing."

While fighting the urge to grab her and shake her, I used my hands in the air in front of me to punctuate every word I loudly said. "But *I* don't want *you*." Taking a deep breath to calm myself, I told her, "Even if we had hooked up that night and even if I had gotten you pregnant, I still wouldn't want you. I'd be there for my kid, but I wouldn't want you. I already have someone in my life and that's not going to change." Though technically right now, I wasn't totally convinced I had Monroe. She'd stood me up for this meeting without a call or a text when she'd been the one to offer to be here.

Hannah snapped back as if I'd actually slapped her and her face began to turn red with what I assumed was anger. "This is only going to get worse for you." Then with disgust she added, "And this supposed person in your life." After taking a moment to glare at me, she asked, "Who is she?"

I shook my head. "That's none of your business."

"I'm about to *make it* my business."

Now I took a step forward. "Is that a threat?" Because no matter how miffed I was at Monroe for today, no matter if she still wanted to be with me, I'd protect her. She didn't deserve to deal with this with everything she was dealing with on her own.

A sly grin spread across her face. "Not at all. I'm just saying this isn't over."

"It is for me." I walked the long way around the table toward the door to avoid getting any closer to her than I had to. "I won't meet with you again and I *will* figure out how to force a paternity test out of you."

"You can't do that." Her voice wavered and for a split second, I felt something like concern for her. Then that feeling disappeared just as quickly. She was the one trying to control my life. "My father will disown me."

I glanced back at her. She was picking at her fingernails and breathing erratically. She was actually concerned, which to me meant whoever had *actually* gotten her pregnant was going to piss her father off enough for him to turn his back on her.

But that was her problem. Not mine.

"That's not my problem," I told her, then I left the room and went directly to Manning's office, as we'd discussed.

He shut the door behind him then went to make sure Hannah had been escorted out of the building before coming back to me so I could tell him everything that had happened.

"That's interesting," he said. "The fact that she said her father would disown her twice leads me to believe that whoever the baby's father is would be a problem for her father. Which is why she latched on to you."

I threw my hands in the air and let them hit the arms of the chair I was sitting in. "That doesn't make sense to me, though, because if I was the better choice, why would her dad trade me? Wouldn't he want to keep me there?"

Manning shook his head. "I can't say what's going through his head, but the fact that she also mentioned that you come from money tells me she's looking for security. We can use that."

I narrowed my eyes on him. "Are you saying you want me to pay her off?"

He chuckled. "Not at all. But information is power, so we can go from there. I'm going to use my private investigator to see if we can figure out who the real father might be. That could help us. I'll also continue to work on a court order for a paternity test. Hopefully, in two weeks when she's far enough along, we can get that blood test done."

"Good."

"Now." He glanced at his watch. "I've got another case I need to deal with right now and you have a game to get to, don't you?"

"Yeah," I told him as I stood.

Technically, I didn't have a game for hours, but

I did have a workout and a bull pen session to throw.

Reaching out my hand, he took it and shook it as I thanked him for his help. Sure, he was getting paid a fuck ton for it, but I still appreciated it.

And maybe the investigator would get to the bottom of this, but right now, I didn't give a fuck. Let her leak it. What would it matter in the end?

Other than the fact that anyone who knew Monroe and that we were together would assume it was true and she'd be inundated with questions.

If we *were* even still fucking together. Her not showing up today sent a message.

On my way home, I went by her apartment and her car wasn't there, so I didn't stop.

Should I have been worried that something had happened to her? I didn't think so. She was spending the morning with her dads, so I wasn't concerned that the fucknut would get to her. If she'd had an accident, I would've been called, I thought.

No. Her not showing up had been a choice. One I'd have to deal with later because right now, I had to get my head in the proverbial game.

Fuck all of this.

My choices were that I could go home or go to Brooks's house.

I chose my brother's place after the game. It was easy to hang out except that I lost track of the number of beers I'd been drinking, which was very much unlike me.

But two things became true.

One, I was going to sleep like the dead.

Two, I was going to regret this night in the morning.

CHAPTER 20
MONROE

"*T*his is honestly beautiful."

I was standing in Papa's shop, looking at an intricate design he'd created on this dining table. It was a beautiful, dark wood with the center carved out of the middle. Instead of a fabric running, these people would have a permanent one that had been hand-carved by my papa.

It looked like a thinner version of the tree of life. Most would think it'd turn into a dust collector, but it wouldn't. After he carved it, he put this special coating on it. Not resin because the entire thing wasn't filled. I was sure of that once I'd run my hand over the carving. Then he turned on the lights that somehow shone up from the bottom.

"It's a masterpiece," Dad told him, then he gave him a kiss.

My dads never shied away from affection just because I was there. Appropriate affection because they were my dads and any more than light pecks would have made me nauseous.

"You know you're going to have to do my entire house when I buy one someday, right?" I said.

He chuckled and nodded. "I do know that. It'll be my pleasure. Assuming your husband even likes my work."

I scoffed. "First of all, who's to say I'm going to buy a house only once I'm married? How do you know I won't buy a house next year? I won't be married next year. Secondly, do you think I'd care who liked what? Your stuff is gorgeous and has a really high resale value, especially for pieces you've done yourself. He'd have to live with it until I sold everything."

Both of my dads were roaring with laughter, knowing that I'd never sell one of Papa's pieces. Though anyone who didn't like his stuff was probably not someone I could be with.

"Nice shirt," Papa said as he flung an arm around me, squeezing me to him.

"I like it." I'd gotten it online. It had Medusa in

the middle and read *The Female Gaze* across the top and *Petrify the Patriarchy* along the bottom.

"Very Monroe," Dad agreed. "All right, both of you. I have to get to work. Meeting in about thirty minutes. I love you both and will see you later." He dropped a kiss to the top of my head, gave Papa another quick one, then hurried out.

As busy as Dad was, he always made time for us.

"Is he going to take time off for your vacation or is he working through it?" I asked as we walked back toward Papa's office.

"Time off. He's not allowed to bring anything with him. Are you still coming with us?" He dropped into his chair at his desk. It was just like the one he had at home and no, it wasn't one of his. There were a ton of his pieces around the house, but he hated doing desks and would usually only design them.

"You know... I don't think so." Even though I wanted to badly. I hadn't been to Hawaii since I was sixteen.

He raised his eyebrows. "No?"

"No." Though it was something I'd decided here in the moment. Originally, I'd been excited when they'd asked and had planned on going. "You two deserve a vacation of your own," I explained. "You always take me and this time it should just be the two of you."

Even when I'd been little, they'd always taken me. Part of that was because there hadn't been anyone close enough to us they'd felt comfortable leaving me with. Part of it was because they'd said they wanted to experience all of it with me. Like my face the first time I'd seen the Eiffel Tower.

There were some short overnights and weekend trips that they'd gone on without me once I'd been older and could stay home alone, but a true vacation? None.

"We love having you with us and now that you're an adult, it's not like having your kid with you."

"But it is still like having a third wheel," I countered. "So no, you two go. I'll handle everything at the house and if you want, I can take messages for work so that everything is organized when you get back."

Because being gone from a business like this was a pain, though Papa had the best assistant known to man. Still, I did need to have something to do this summer now that I didn't have to work to pay for the damage to Owen's car.

"We'll think of something." But then he needed to get to work, so I was going to head home to change before I met up with Cobb for his meeting with the not-baby-mama.

"Um, so do you want to tell your friend that I don't need the job anymore or should I call him?" I asked but then quickly added, "I should call him right? That's the grown up thing to do?"

Papa chuckled. "It is but he's coming in here this afternoon. I'll tell him. Since he hadn't fit you in yet, I don't think he'll be upset."

"Thank you, Papa." I hurried over and wrapped my arms around his shoulders. "I love you."

"I love you, too. Now get out of here so I can get some work done."

Which was exactly what I did.

I was only about two miles from home when the lights began flashing behind me. Moving the car over, I hoped the cop just wanted to get past me, but nope. He pulled over behind me.

"What the hell?" I muttered. I hadn't been speeding, hadn't run any lights or signs that I knew of. This didn't make any sense.

Now, I had to wait.

The officer approached the car the way they

always do. With caution and suspicion since they never know what they're going to find. And Dad had taught me how to handle these things over the years and what I actually had to comply with. So I sat there with my hands on the steering wheel and waited.

"Roll the window down," he said through the glass. It wasn't until he'd spoken that I reached over and hit the button. "License."

I blew out a breath. This was how it was going to work.

As I grabbed my purse, making slow, purposeful movements so that he wouldn't get spooked, and pulled my wallet out, I ask, "What am I being pulled over for?"

"License," he repeated.

I couldn't get a good look at him. He was tall enough but probably didn't reach six feet and was in good shape if his arms had anything to say about it. Almost as soon as I handed him my ID, he said, "Step out of the car, please."

While trying not to panic, I stepped out of my car.

"Monroe Phillips?" he asked and I knew he was just confirming it. "You're under arrest."

I furrowed my brows and said, "Under arrest? What did I do?"

"I'll explain everything once I search you."

In the times that I'd been arrested, I'd been searched by a woman at the police station because I'd been arrested for protesting. The last time, it had again been a woman who'd done a very quick search at the site then done a more thorough one at the station.

But this man had me turn around and put my hands on the trunk of my car.

"Can we please request a female officer?" I asked because I could.

"None available."

Which didn't surprise me. He ran his hands over me. Luckily, I was wearing shorts and a T-shirt with sandals, so there wasn't much area to search. He used the backs of his hands to go under my breasts and between them. And to go over any other sensitive areas. He did what he was supposed to do and there wasn't anything creepy about it, but it still made me uncomfortable and I would've preferred a woman.

"Can you tell me why I'm being arrested now?" I asked when he turned me back around.

"Destruction of private property."

I punched my brows together in confusion. "Whose property?"

"They'll explain it at the station."

"Can we take my purse, please?" Because my car was going to get towed and who knew when I'd get it back. "And my phone?"

At first it looked like the cop was going to say *no*, but then he grabbed my purse but when he went to shove it into my purse, he missed and the phone fell to the ground and the sound of shattering glass made me cringe. My poor phone. Then he leaned in and turned my car off, leaving the keys. A second car showed up. I was put into the back seat of the second car and taken away. The original officer would have to deal with my car.

I dropped my head back onto the headrest and kept my mouth shut as my father had told me to do. He said never answer questions or offer any explanation. At least not until he was there. That was exactly what I did.

Sitting in a holding cell—again, with my knee bouncing because I was missing the meeting with Cobb today and couldn't even call him to tell him.

"Ready for your phone call?" The woman officer asked outside the holding cell.

"Yes, please."

Luckily, she didn't put handcuffs on me again. If I never had another pair of those on me, it'd be too soon. But then there was the dilemma.

Realistically, I knew I had to call my dad. He was the one who could help me. But my heart wanted to call Cobb so at least he'd know that I hadn't stood him up. This was beyond my control. Not to mention, I didn't actually know Cobb's number from memory.

My dad's, I did.

He picked up on the second ring, probably used to seeing calls from jail come up on his caller ID.

"Jonathan Phillips," he answered, his voice strong. I'd have to brace for the disappointment I was about to hear.

"Dad," I said.

He sighed into the phone. "Monroe?"

"I'm going to need some help."

"Clearly."

Another thing Dad had explained was to not say much on the phones in any jail or prison because they were monitored. He covered the phone and spoke to someone on his end, then came back and said, "I'll be right there. Don't say anything."

Then he hung up without waiting for a response.

Back in the cell, I sat, knee bouncing again, knowing that Dad was going to be pissed when he got here, though he wouldn't show it. He'd believe me, I reminded myself. I had to believe he would. I'd never lied to him about why I was arrested before or really about anything and I wouldn't start now. Hopefully that long history would pay off here.

The woman reappeared to take me to an interview room. This was where I'd get to talk to my dad before I was questioned by police. I'd made it clear I wouldn't answer anything without my lawyer. I'd said that right away so they wouldn't even keep asking.

"Monroe," Dad said as soon as I'd gotten into the room. I ran into his arms, where he held me tightly. For some reason, this arrest scared me. "What'd you do?"

I pulled away. "Nothing. Destruction of private property, apparently, but I don't even know whose property I supposedly destroyed."

Dad pursed his lips and cocked his head to the side. "Sure you do. Owen's."

I stepped back then began to pace. "When did I supposedly do that?"

"This morning," he said.

"I didn't do anything, Dad. I was with Cobb in my apartment, then alone there, then Papa's shop with you, then on my way home, then here. I don't seek him out." My eyes burned with tears. "Why is he doing this?"

"Well, he clearly has a problem." Dad sat at the table and motioned for me to do the same across from him. "But we'll deal with that." He pulled his tablet out of his bag. "The complaint says that you showed up, were jealous because he was with another woman, then basically lost your shit. Kicked the door until it broke, shattered a few windows, left tire marks on the yard."

I narrowed my eyes. "Where would I do that? He lives in an apartment."

"His parents' house."

Shaking my head, I told him, "I don't even know where his parents live."

"Several of his friends gave statements saying it was you." He glanced up at me. "This isn't great, but I think if we can piece things together by the minute, we'll be fine. But you have to let me file an order against him, Monroe. This is ridiculous and I'm not waiting for him to escalate."

"Yeah," I told him. "You can do that." Because at this point, I needed something to back me up.

"I have the video from the ring camera from the night he showed up. I saved it just in case. That alone should be enough to show that he's the one with the problem here."

"Good. But what about today? I'm supposed to be meeting Cobb…" I flipped his phone around so that I could see the time and groaned. "In twenty minutes."

Dad shook his head. "That's not going to happen. I'm going to work on this now, but it's going to take a little bit. I'll go see the prosecutor to work this out and file the protection order so he has to stay away from you."

"I will be waiting patiently," I said. Dad scowled. "OK, not patiently." Dad got up but I'd have to wait right where I was for the officer to come get me.

"I'll be back soon."

Then Dad was gone and I was spent staring at the gray floor of the holding cell for hours.

It was almost dinner time when the door

opened again and Dad peeked his head through. "We're good to go."

I hopped up so quickly and hurried out that door. I never wanted to get arrested again.

The sun was still bright when I stepped out. We were headed to Dad's car since mine had been impounded. It wasn't until we were inside his car that I asked any questions due to him telling me over and over to always assume someone was listening in public spaces.

"So… what happened?" I asked.

"With everything about your morning, the ring camera showing you leave, Papa and I being able to vouch for you at the shop—along with security cameras there—the prosecutor agrees that the time-line doesn't work. There's no way you could be at Owen's parents' house on the south side."

My eyes widened. I would've had to be fucking Houdini with a magical unicorn to make it out there, destroy some property, and get back in the amount of time I had unaccounted for this morning.

"The officer who pulled you over was on his way to your apartment to arrest you. He just happened to see you before he got there."

"Lucky timing." I rolled my eyes. "So it's done?"

"Yeah. They sent a couple of officers out to talk to Owen. He might get arrested for filing a false report. Mostly, I asked them to scare him into leaving you alone."

"Officers you know?" I asked. He nodded. "That figures." And was also a reason I never broke any laws outside of being arrested at protests. But as a teenager, I'd never known which cops my dad knew and which he didn't. Also, it hadn't mattered because he'd find out what I'd been doing, anyway. And my dads had never given me a reason to rebel.

"Also, the officer who took the complaint is the same one who arrested you. Turns out, he's Owen's cousin," Dad said. I didn't understand why that was significant. "Without going into it, let's just say that not everything in the report was accurate, so he's getting his wrist slapped for that. And has been highly encouraged to make it clear to Owen that he needs to leave you alone."

"And the protection order?" My stomach clenched at the idea of getting one. There were too many horror stories about women who got one and all it did was trigger the guy. I just didn't want to deal with him.

"I've filed, but it takes time. Since he never actually hit you…" Dad looked at me with raised brows.

I shook my head. He was an asshole, but he hadn't hit me. "It might not be top priority. Honestly, I don't know that I can make a convincing stalking allegation, either, since this is sporadic and he's not showing up where you are that we know of."

"OK." I blew out a breath. "We'll just see what happens with this, then."

"Yeah. And don't worry. This arrest won't be on your record."

I snickered. There was enough there already. "And my car?"

"Oh, right. We'll have to pick that up. They were already processing it, so it'll be tomorrow."

"Fine by me. I'm not leaving my apartment tonight."

"Oh, your phone was broken." I'd been afraid of that when I heard the glass shatter. "It won't even turn on."

"So I need to get a new one."

He nodded. "I'll get you a new one tonight."

"Thanks, Dad."

Because there seemed to be the safest place for me right now. How did I know if I walked out of the house, I wouldn't be arrested again? I didn't even call Cobb because by now, he was at the game. I'd wait until he called me after.

Instead, I ordered some Chinese food from Dad's phone before he left to get me a new one and plopped myself in front of my TV to watch the Knights game. Every once in a while, the camera would show the dugout and my stomach would clench. Cobb was normally relax as he sat watching the game, but tonight his jaw was tense, like he was clenching his teeth and he looked… unhappy.

Which made me really want to know what the hell had happened at that meeting.

I took a deep breath to calm my racing heart.

Hopefully, he'd come to my apartment after and I could find out then.

Cobb couldn't call me after the game because if he did, it'd go right to voicemail. By the time I realized he wasn't going to, it was late enough that I knew he wasn't coming here. He needed his sleep and didn't stay up late.

Dad hadn't brought me the new phone which probably meant he'd also gotten in late and figured he'd give it to me in the morning.

I'd have to deal with it tomorrow.

CHAPTER 21
MONROE

*C*obb hadn't come over after his game last night.

I'd stayed up for quite a while waiting, yet he never showed up. Maybe I should've gone into my dads' house and called him. By the time the thought had occurred to me, it was late, and I didn't want to wake him not to mention his number was in my phone. I might not have known a ton about how being a professional baseball player worked, but he'd told me that the day before he pitched was almost as important as the day he actually pitched. Without the workout the day before, he could get hurt.

No one wanted that.

Once I thought it was a respectable time, I went

into the house and found the phone Dad got me on the kitchen counter with a note saying it was taken care of and called him, hoping he'd answer so I could explain what had happened yesterday. Explain why I'd stood him up for that meeting. It wasn't because I'd wanted to, that was for sure.

The more I thought about the fact that I hadn't shown up and that he didn't know why made me think that was what he was pissed about during the game.

But why hadn't he reached out to see what had happened?

Was it something with that woman? He'd been meeting with her to hopefully figure out a way to end the whole thing. I trusted him, so I didn't think he'd suddenly fallen in love with her, but something must've happened.

After the third time of me trying to call him and him not answering, I sent a text. When he didn't answer that, I decided to drive to his apartment to see if he was home.

Though once I was standing outside of his door, I was less confident.

I took a deep breath then blew it out before knocking. Once I did that, I couldn't scurry away like a scared rabbit the way I wanted to.

No one came to the door.

Without thinking about it, I used the key I still had to his place and let myself in.

"Cobb?" I called out because if he was there and hadn't heard my knock, I didn't want to startle him. Also, somewhere in the back of my mind, I realized that I also didn't want to walk in on something I didn't want to see.

I wasn't sure what that was, but I didn't want it, anyway.

Cheating? No. Cobb wasn't that guy. Yet that little, nagging morsel of doubt still wiggled in the back of my mind. After all that bravado about not worrying about someone cheating on me, that little nugget was there.

First, I checked the bathroom, but he wasn't in there. The door was open and the light was off. Then it was the bedroom, but again, it was empty. Honestly, the bed didn't look like it'd been slept in, which I didn't love.

Swallowing back the uncertainty, my sudden thirst battled with the tenseness in my stomach. Promising myself that I wouldn't let my imagination run wild, I hurried out of his room and his apartment, making sure the door locked behind me.

Then I went right home. It was the only place I

wanted to be. Yet even surrounded by my own things, in the comfort of my own home, it wasn't enough.

I needed my dads.

But I'd have to painfully wait hours until they were home.

Finally, I heard one of their cars and rushed through the door that attached to the house to meet whomever it was in the entryway.

Papa had just dropped his keys in the bowl on the table they used for that.

"Hey, honey. Wasn't expecting to see you there," he said. My bottom lip trembled at the comfort his voice brought. His eyebrows slammed down. "What's going on, Monroe?"

That was too much. I rushed into his arms, which he wrapped snugly around me.

I wasn't going to cry, I told myself. I wasn't. This was just Cobb and me missing each other. But again, that tiny niggling of self-doubt reared its ugly head.

"Monroe?"

"Just hug me." My voice was muffled into his chest.

So we stood there, Papa holding me tightly with my arms wrapped around him. Actually, I hadn't talk to him after I'd been arrested yesterday and assumed Dad had told him everything.

Then the door opened again and without looking, it had to be Dad.

"What's going on?" he whispered. Papa shrugged, which brought Dad over where he wrapped his arms around the both of us. Then he kissed the top of my head and released me, as did Papa. "Monroe?"

I took a deep breath and blew it out slowly. At least I hadn't started to cry. "I think this calls for sushi," I told him. Since I hadn't eaten all day, it was probably time that I did.

Too much of being alone in my apartment had my head swirling and there was no one better to unswirl it than my dads.

"I'll order," Papa said, heading to the kitchen. That was where our takeout menus were.

"Want to talk about it now?" Dad asked.

I shook my head. "I don't want to do it twice."

Papa was back a few minutes later. "Why don't we get changed and Monroe can get drinks? We'll eat in the living room."

"Seriously?" Dad asked.

"It's comfortable and the game's coming on."

He winced. "If we're still watching the game tonight."

I snickered. "We should watch the game."

My dads loved baseball, but they loved me more and if they were thinking something had happened with Cobb—which it sort of had—they'd never watch it with me in the room again if that was what I wanted.

While they went to change, I set us up in the living room. They were only gone fifteen minutes and I'd already turned on the channel for the game. Right now, it was the preshow, where these chumps made all their predictions.

"How was work?" I asked them both once they'd gotten comfortable on the couch. I sat on the floor at the end of the table with my back against the chair.

"The usual," Papa said. "Busy. The couple who bought the table I showed you two yesterday came in to see it. They're very happy. It'll be delivered to them tomorrow."

"That's good." I took a long drink from my pop. "How much did that cost them?"

A sly smile turned the corners of Papa's mouth up. "An embarrassing amount that I'm not going to tell you."

I snorted. He almost never told me how much he charged for custom pieces. Or rather, he didn't tell me outright. It wasn't hard to put together from conversations, though. "And you, Dad?"

"A headache," he said, which was his answer a large amount of the time.

"Why do you do it, then?"

"Because I'm good at it," he countered. "I love the law. Love making sure trials are fair. Don't always love the system."

Wasn't that the truth.

"Did Papa tell you that I'm not going to Hawaii with the two of you?"

"Yes."

The doorbell rang and Dad was about to get up, but Papa said, "I've got it." It had to have been the food. The sushi place was just up the street.

"Change your mind?" Dad asked. "About Hawaii?"

I shook my head. "You two deserve a vacation alone. But I love that you always want me there."

"Always." He watched me for a second as Papa came back in the room and started pulling containers from the bag. He'd ordered me my regular California roll plate, which made me do a little dance in my seat. "Hawaii would be a great place to get over a heartbreak."

Not surprisingly, they thought this was about Cobb breaking my heart. Which wasn't exactly the truth.

"No. No. No heartbreak here," I assured them. "Papa, did Dad tell you everything about yesterday?"

"Yeah. He filled me in on the whole thing. That fucker better stay away from you." My dads almost never swore, so when they did, it was startling.

"I think he will," Dad told him. "He's getting other people in trouble now. His cousin has a ding in his file even though he claims he just took the report. The report wasn't correct." That was the cop who had arrested me. "And I reached out to his uncle, the deputy mayor. He assured me that he'd take care of it."

"Will he be charged?" Papa asked.

Dad shrugged and took a drink of his beer. "Don't know yet. His uncle might get it brushed under the rug. We'll see."

"You know, Monroe, it's sometimes better to let things slide," Papa said before putting a bite in his mouth.

I shook my head and swallowed the last of the

roll I had in my mouth. "No can do. Not when someone's harassing a gay couple."

"It's still better to let it go sometimes."

"I'll see what I can do." But we all knew there was zero chance that I was going to do that in the future. If for now, Dad got Owen off my ass, I'd at least pretend.

"So what's going on?" Dad asked more gently.

I took a breath and set my chopsticks down. "I haven't heard from Cobb."

"Since when?"

"Night before last," I told them. "I was supposed to meet him at the coffee shop yesterday to go to a meeting with him, but I was in a holding cell."

"Have you called him?" Papa asked.

"This morning. I didn't have my phone last night remember? I even went to his apartment and the bed didn't even look slept in." That was the part that was bothering me the most.

Dad pointed at the TV. "He's clearly fine."

I swung my head in the direction of the TV and sure enough, there was video of Cobb throwing pitches in the bull pen. The announcer guy said it was from his session earlier and he wasn't sure what was going on with Cobb, but a fire had been lit and he was throwing harder than ever.

It was probably anger.

"What kind of meeting?" Dad asked as he turned the volume down.

"Well, you were both there when I heard about the baby mama drama."

"We were." Papa sat his container on the table, more interested in what I was about to say than the food. "I've been waiting for you to tell us what the hell that was about."

"Well… It's not *his* baby mama drama. There's a woman who says she is pregnant by him, but he swears he never touched her," I explained. My dads glanced at each other. I could read those looks. "I know how it sounds, but I trust him."

"OK," Dad said, but his tone told me that he didn't believe me. Why would he? He didn't know Cobb.

"A paternity test will prove it," I explained.

"Good."

"Anyway, I didn't show up and he's not answering my calls. Went to his apartment, but he wasn't there." I sighed. "I don't know. I thought we were together, but maybe I misunderstood."

"You do have a knack for picking the wrong men," Dad teased.

"And I don't get it," Papa continued. "With the prime examples you grew up with, it's kind of weird."

I rolled my eyes. "*One* wrong man. One. And I only dated him for, like, a month. It's not my fault he's got this weird obsession or whatever."

Dad's face darkened. "That's not really something to joke about."

"I know. I just… I wish Cobb would answer the phone."

Papa pushed up so that he was sitting on the edge of the couch and rested his elbows on his knees. "He probably can't, honey. He's working."

That was true, but he wouldn't have been working this morning.

But I also didn't want to talk about it with them anymore and continued eating my sushi.

My heart jumped every single time the camera showed Cobb on the screen.

If I didn't hear from him tonight, I'd be on his doorstep first thing in the morning.

CHAPTER 22
COBB

*N*ow that it was clear that Hannah wasn't going to stop, it was time to ask for some help. The lawyer had said he was going to get an investigator on it and he was the one she'd sent me to. Now it was time to see if there was anything more she could do.

After all, as the acting owner of the Knights, she likely had a relationship of some kind with Doug Johnson, the owner of my former team and Hannah's father. Maybe she could knock some sense into them.

Which was how I found myself at my parents' house bright and early. I had to get this shit taken care of before I had to be at the park for warmup. I was starting today.

I didn't knock before I went into their house. We never did even once we'd all moved out.

Mom and Dad were both at the dining table eating their breakfast when she looked up and saw me headed their way.

"This is an unexpected surprise," Mom said as she set her coffee cup on the table.

Dad looked up from his phone and frowned. Totally expected. "Do I know you?" he asked, likely because I hadn't seen him since I'd been back. Now, it hadn't been that long and he'd been out of town, but he'd still bust my balls over it.

"I think you were there when I was born," I told him. "Unless you pussed out and waited in the waiting room."

Mom snorted. "He was there."

Dad had played out of Kalamazoo when I'd been born, so there wouldn't have been an excuse to miss the birth, especially since I'd been born in the off season. All of us had been.

"Ah, yes. The fourth person I saw come out of your mother."

I cringed. "There had to be a better way to say that."

Mom shook her head and patted the table with her hand. Something she did when she wanted us to sit down. I pulled out the chair across from her, which left Dad at the head of the table. "What's going on? It's unusual for you to be here this early and on a day you start."

"I met with Hannah Johnson yesterday at Manning's office."

Mom took a breath, probably steeling herself for what was to come, but Dad grunted.

"I told all of you boys that women are just going to get you into trouble." His phone hit the table harder than it needed to.

Yeah. He had said that. Our entire lives. If it were up to that man, each of his sons would just find a woman to fuck when we needed a release and move on from there. No attachments and always wear a condom so we didn't end up in the very situation I was in.

Not to mention the stories that were out there about what he'd been like when he was young and played. That would've been before he'd met my mother. Or rather before they'd been a thing. Whatever.

"You've made your opinion clear." I lightly tapped my fingers on the table. Dad didn't make me nervous, but I was anxious to get this whole mess taken care of. "In this case, you'll be happy to know that I didn't fuck her."

Dad winced. "There had to be a better way to say that."

I snorted. Dad had the biggest potty mouth of any of us except maybe Camden, which was saying something. He just didn't like any of us to use it around my mother. For whatever reason, no matter how shitty of a dad he was, he seemed to really love my mother.

"Well," I told him, "I didn't. And trust me, we all heard the *wrap it before you tap it* talks our entire fucking lives. I don't take chances."

Dad shrugged. "That's not one hundred percent."

"It's not." I fucking hated telling him he was right. "But you know what is? The fact that I never touched her."

Mom sighed and shook her head. She might've been used to this kind of back and forth with us, but that didn't mean she liked it. "What do you need, sweetheart?"

I sat up straighter and wet my lips. "You know Doug Johnson, right?"

"I know him. We have a cordial relationship."

"Can you talk to him? Get him to figure his

daughter out so she'll leave me alone?" I asked. Mom's mouth opened like she was going to answer and I wasn't going to like it, so I kept talking. "Listen, she said she thinks her dad will disown her if he finds out who the real father is."

"She said that?" Dad asked. "She said you're not the father? Did anyone hear that?"

"No." I shook my head. "It was a stipulation of the meeting. She wanted us to be alone, probably for that reason."

Dad grunted again.

"Anyway…" I focused back on Mom. "This isn't going well otherwise. She's not going to stop. Pretty sure she's going to start talking to the press, which affects all of us."

"If you'd let me answer a second ago, I would've told you that of course I'll help you. I'll reach out to him today and see what we can figure out." She took a drink of her coffee.

"Thank you." It was like a weight had been lifted off my shoulders.

"He's not an easy man to contend with. I don't have an issue, but I can see where his daughter would have more problems. That doesn't excuse what she's doing to you. I should have an answer later today."

"Thanks, Mom."

I was about to get up and head back home when Mom asked, "How is Monroe? That's her name, right? The woman you're seeing?" And my stomach tightened again. All of my muscles tensed. "It's not easy to keep a secret in this family, Cobb. You know that."

And I sighed. "I'm not sure. She was supposed to be there for that meeting—she wasn't going in. She never showed up."

Mom's brows slammed down. "Is she OK? Did something happen?"

"I don't know," I told her honestly, even though my father was sitting right there and would have an opinion about it. "I didn't talk to her after. I had to throw my session. Then the game. Then I went to Brooks's house, had a bit too much to drink, and my phone died."

"You didn't drive home, did you, Cobb?"

"Of course not. I stayed there. I'm on my way home to pack my bag now."

"So call her now."

"It's early," I told her. "I don't know. She stood me up. Maybe we don't have what I thought we did."

Mom's eyes widened. "So it's getting serious?"

"I thought it was."

"Big mistake," Dad said, which was totally expected. "You're in your prime. There's no reason to get caught up with some woman."

Mom rolled her eyes. "You don't even know her."

"I don't have to," he countered. "Now is not the time for any of this. Look at Silas with the Kincaid girl. He's been torn up over her for years."

"He felt guilty," I told him. "Like he was responsible for her brother's death."

"I know that," he snapped. "Which was ridiculous and it might've held him back. Now, Urban with…"

I sighed. "Everly."

"Right. Bringing women in now is a big mistake. Take after Brooks and wait until you're done with baseball. It doesn't last forever."

"Well," I said as I pushed up from the chair. "Some of us can't help who we love, Dad. It's called being human. I understand that might not be your thing, but the rest of us kind of prefer it. Whether I'm with Monroe or not, baseball is my job—not my life."

"It needs to be your life if you want to succeed."

I'd already started walking toward the door. "I think we're all doing pretty well already."

Then I shut the door behind me because I didn't want to hear another word he had to say.

All of us had a slightly different way of dealing with our father. Brooks was picky with when he was going to argue and when he wasn't. Silas only responded when he absolutely had to. Urban used avoiding the man to begin with. I normally just walked out when he was getting to be too much and my trigger on that was quick.

Camden, on the other hand, argued every fucking thing with man. I admired that but at the same time knew it was a waste.

When I got back to my apartment, after plugging my dead phone in, I realized I'd left my bag at the park. It was fine, though annoying. I had another one and was actively packing it when there was a knock at my door.

Standing on the other side was Monroe. Her strawberry hair was down in wild waves and she was wearing jean shorts, a Knights T-shirt, and tennis shoes. She looked perfect for a game. It wasn't until she'd cleared her throat that I realized I hadn't said a word to let her in. So I stepped back so she could enter.

Monroe had her arms folded under her breasts and honestly, I wanted to drag her to the floor and sink into her right where we were.

"Hey," I finally said.

"Hi." She turned to me and wet her bottom lip. I leaned my ass against the back of my couch and rested my hands beside me.

She waited. When I didn't say anything she sighed. "I guess in the interest of full disclosure I should tell you that I used the key you gave me yesterday and came here. You weren't here."

"That's fine." It was, after all, the reason that I'd given her the key. "I didn't come home last night. Actually, I wasn't here anytime after I left for the meeting."

Monroe sighed and nodded her head. "Didn't you want to know why I didn't meet you?"

"Of course I did," I snapped. "But after the meeting, I had to get to the park. I had to throw my bull pen session, then another one yesterday, because I'm starting today."

"And after?"

"I went to Brooks's, had too much to drink because I was pissed, then slept there."

"And this morning?"

I furrowed my brows. "I went to talk to my

mom. Then I came here. Why do you want to know every single thing I did?" I wasn't accusing her of anything. It was just weird because Monroe had never asked for this much detail.

She shook her head and looked away. "Weren't you at all curious why I didn't meet you?"

"Obviously. Honestly, I assumed that the conversation the night before was too much and you didn't want to deal with it." I sighed. "Yesterday, I had a lot of shit to deal with. I had to throw. There was team shit. I had to recover from a hangover. Do you know how long it's been since I had a hangover? I felt like garbage yesterday."

"You know what they say when you assume," she muttered then took a deep breath. "No. I don't know how long it's been since you had a hangover. But I was *arrested* two days ago, Cobb. So I couldn't meet you because I was in jail all of the day. The cop broke my phone. You didn't answer when I called."

"What?" I stood to my full height, mentally kicking my own ass. I'd gotten so lost in dealing with my own shit that I'd almost forgotten that she had her own. "Arrested for what?"

She threw her hands in the air. "Apparently, I destroyed some private property, even though I was at Papa's shop then was stopped on my way home. When I had to time to do it, no idea."

"Hang on." I closed the distance between us. "We need to talk about this. Do you want a drink?"

She shook her head, then I led her over to the couch so we could both sit down. I turned with one leg on the cushion so that I'd be facing her. She did the same thing.

"So, back up," I told her. "You were arrested."

"Yes. I was on my way home to change to meet you and was stopped. Then I was arrested because I destroyed some private property."

"Whose?"

She scowled at me. "Whose do you think? Ex-dickhead."

My stomach burned with anger. This fucker was going way too far. I ran a hand down my face. "I'm going to have kill him."

She snorted. "I'd help dispose of the body, but no. You don't. It's handled, but I spent the entire day in a damn holding cell. Dad got me out of it and is pretty sure he's putting an end to things." She sighed. "The cop who arrested me is his cousin. That cousin's dad is the deputy mayor." I groaned. "So Dad had a chat with the deputy mayor."

"So you're good? Are you all right?"

"I am, but I was kind of curious why the man I thought was my boyfriend wasn't worried when I didn't show up."

Well, fuck me. I was the asshole here. "I got caught up in my own shit. Made some assumptions…" I groaned. "Like I said, I was fucked up yesterday."

She eyed me cautiously. "I think I made some assumptions of my own that were wrong."

Pushing my fingers into her hair, I cupped her cheek. "You weren't wrong. At least if you're talking about me being yours. I am. I was… tied up all day the day of the meeting and all fucked up yesterday. It's not an excuse, but that's what happened. My phone died the night I was at Brooks'. Charged it once I got to the field but you know I don't keep it on me when I throw."

"Yeah, what's that about? I thought none of you drank much."

"We don't… It wasn't a normal thing." I traced my thumb over her cheekbone. "Tell me what happened."

I set my hand on her back to rub small circles while she told me everything that had happened with her arrest and after.

"I tried calling you an embarrassing number of times," she finally said.

"There's no such thing. Fuck, I'm sorry, Monroe. I let my anger get the best of me."

She gave me a small nod, but I wasn't sure that was an acceptance. "Now tell me about your meeting. All the details."

So I did. Every single thing about that meeting, Monroe now knew.

"You walked away? Leaving her there?"

I nodded, but the way Monroe swallowed didn't sit right with me. "Wait. Did you think I was going to leave with her? The woman trying to control my life?"

She looked away quickly. "Of course not."

Slowly, I brought her face back toward me so that I could see her. "Monroe?"

She sighed. "No. Not really. I mean maybe there was a tiny split second of doubt which isn't at all like me, but not now."

"I wouldn't cheat on you, Monroe. I've never cheated on anyone in my life."

Her shoulders slumped. "It was my self-doubt. Not anything about you. I think…" She sighed. "I think that whole thing I said about not bothering with jealousy was because I never had anyone I cared about enough to be jealous. I don't like it. It doesn't feel good even if it's only a teeny tiny bit." She pushed her index finger and thumb close together to where only daylight could fit through to illustrate how much jealousy she'd felt.

Releasing my leg, I turned my body so that I was sitting normally, then reached over and brought her onto my lap facing me. I wrapped my arms around her and brought her mouth to mine. I wanted this kiss to convey everything I felt about her. Maybe it was too soon to tell her that I loved her, but I fucking did. That was why her not showing up yesterday had cut so deeply.

All of this was my fault. I called her right away but she didn't answer. Now I knew it was because she was in jail but at the time, I figured she just didn't want to talk to me and I wasn't about to force the woman to do anything she didn't want. No matter how pissed I'd been, I shouldn't have let it make my decisions for me.

The way she held on to my shoulders, her hips slightly moving, had me as hard as a rock and though I didn't want to, I had to bring the kiss to an end.

"If I cheated on you, Monroe, I'd lose you and I never want to lose you."

She looked up at me with those beautiful, blue eyes. "So we're together."

"We already decided that."

Her teeth sunk into her bottom lip, then she let it go. "I need it to be clear."

"We're together," I told her. "I'm so fucking yours until the day you tell me you don't want me to be."

"That day won't come," she whispered.

"Perfect."

Then I claimed her lips again.

Monroe slipped her hands under my shirt, making me groan.

If I could have, I would've taken her right then. I supposed there was always later.

CHAPTER 23
MONROE

Feeling Cobb underneath me gave me the most powerful feeling. I was in control and it was a heady thing. His hands ran up my sides and I couldn't stop myself from basically dry-humping him right there on the couch. In about two seconds, it was going to be wet-humping.

I was already wet. We just needed to get rid of all of these clothes.

When I leaned back and pulled my shirt over my head, Cobb groaned and let his head fall back.

"I can't," he said, which made me smile and slide myself over his erection.

"I think you can."

His big hand cupped my cheek then slid down my chest, almost purposefully avoiding my breasts.

"I really can't," he said with so much regret. "First, there's not nearly enough time for everything I want to do to you. Second, I can't fuck you right before I start. That'll mess me up."

I hadn't thought of that.

Realizing what he meant, I slid back quickly and crossed my arms over my chest. Why? I didn't know. I was still covered by my bra.

"Sorry," I told him.

He slowly pulled my arms away from me. "No reason to be sorry. I really wish I didn't have a game today." He ran his hands over me. "Fuck. This might mess me up, anyway. It's all I'm going to be thinking about."

"Picture Brooks naked when you pitch to him."

He groaned and ran a hand over his face. "Mood thoroughly killed."

Snickering, I hopped off his lap and pulled my shirt back on. Reluctantly, he got up as well.

"You're coming to the game?"

"I didn't have a plan," I told him honestly. "I wasn't sure how this was going to go."

He cocked his head to the side. "So, you're coming to the game?"

Now that made me laugh. "Yeah, I'm coming to the game. It's the first time I'll see you pitch live."

"And if I fuck up, you'll know it's your fault."

I dropped my mouth open. "How dare you."

"Come on," he said once he'd stopped laughing as he grabbed my hand. "I have to pack my bag. You can come with me."

Inside his room, I kicked off my shoes, which I normally did at the door. I hadn't this time because I hadn't known I was staying. Then I climbed up onto his bed and settled myself right in the middle with my legs out straight in front of me. A black duffle bag sat on the end of the bed.

"Fuck." He sighed. "I like seeing you in my bed. I really wish we didn't have a game."

I shrugged. "But we have after the game, right?"

"Yes, we fucking do."

"What are you packing?" Some of this was still very new to me.

"Anything I might need while I'm at the park. Clothes for after I shower. That kind of thing."

"You don't just put what you're wearing back on?"

"Sometimes, but I'm not putting dirty underwear back on."

Yeah, that made sense. We continued like that until the bag was done and he zipped it up. Then he crawled over me.

"You're not supposed to be doing this," I said, though my breathing had already quickened.

"You're too tempting."

"I'm just sitting here."

Cobb dropped his head to my chest and asked, "Do you want me to leave a ticket at will call?"

"Can I let you know?" I asked. "I'll see if my dads are going. I can always tag along with them."

"Then leave with me after?"

"Absolutely."

Unfortunately, no matter how badly the two of us wanted to stay like we were, he had to get to the field. After walking me to my car, he headed to his.

My dads were planning on going to the game and hadn't invited anyone else, so they had a ticket for me.

We were driving to the field when Dad said, "I heard back from Owen's uncle today."

"You did?" My stomach tightened and there were butterflies suddenly flapping around my chest and not the good kind you got when your crush talked to you.

"I did. It's handled. You shouldn't hear from him again."

I furrowed my brows. "Did you have him killed?"

Papa laughed, but Dad said, "Jesus Christ, Monroe, no. I explained to the uncle that we'd not only file a protection order, but I'd sue the hell out of him for harassment. He's not going to be charged for filing the false report, which I wanted him to be, but for the same of this being over, I'm going to let it go. I also mentioned releasing the doorbell camera. It's an election year, so…"

"Well, good. Whatever it takes to get him to leave me alone," I said. Dad hit the brakes hard, sending me into the back of Papa's seat. "For the record, I wasn't against you having him killed. I would just want to know about it."

Papa continued to laugh, but Dad let out a frustrated groan. "Don't say that stuff to me. I really don't want to have to defend you."

I scoffed. "I didn't say *I* would have him killed."

Figuring that was enough torture of my dads for the night, I sat back and enjoyed the ride. I even remembered to grab the lanyard pass that Camden had given me before, which meant I could go down to wait near the clubhouse for Cobb after the game because one thing was for sure.

I wasn't going home with my dads.

Camden glanced back as we took our seats and

waved. I'd heard that everyone liked her and it made sense. She was an easy person to like.

"So you're all good with Cobb?" Papa asked.

"I'm *all* good with Cobb. We worked it out."

"You don't have to say it like that," Dad countered, causing Papa to chuckle.

My brows pinched together. "Say it like what?"

"I'm *all* good." He made it sound so suggestive.

"That's disgusting," I said seriously and shook my head at him. I wasn't serious, but this made it funnier.

Both teams came out to line the baseline for the national anthem and we all stood as well. It was my first glimpse of Cobb since I'd left his apartment earlier.

Can we just all appreciate baseball uniforms?

"Baseball pants are nice, aren't they?" Papa whispered, which made me focus on something else entirely.

"Dad's going to kill you," I whispered back. But then the music played and we both quieted down.

The girl they had singing it today couldn't have been more than fourteen and she belted out those notes like she'd been doing it her entire life. It was amazing. At the end, most of the place cheered.

But the team headed back to their dugout.

Cobb looked up and saw me. The corners of his mouth turned up as he nodded and his teeth sunk into his bottom lip. Heat *whooshed* over me.

The man was beautiful and the fact that he seemed to only have eyes for me made my knees weak.

As we were sitting back down, Papa said, "Well, you can't deny that was adorable."

"Pft," Dad responded. "I can."

"Oh, come on, Jonathan," he said with laughter in his voice.

"What?" He took a drink of his beer. "I can deny anything I want."

"The man clearly cares about our daughter."

"We'll see."

I sighed. Papa was the more romantic of the two and Dad was always skeptical. Probably came with his profession, but even I could hear that there was humor in Dad's voice.

Cobb was on the mound throwing some practice pitches. He'd stretch his shoulders and neck every couple of pitches.

And the game began.

I'd never fully appreciated baseball before this moment. Watching the guys play was awe inspiring. The fact that they they'd all built their bodies up with the power to do what they were doing... Amazing.

By the third inning, Cobb hadn't given up a hit, though Kalamazoo had two runs. Every time Cobb threw a ball, the smack of it against Brooks's glove startled me.

"Doesn't that hurt Brooks's hand?" I asked.

"Nah," Papa said. "He has a special glove, remember?" The last couple of weeks, I'd been asking a lot of questions and learning a ton. I'd learned over the years, but not like since I'd met Cobb.

"Right. But Cobb throws hard, doesn't he?"

"He does. If you look up there." He pointed to the score board. "The number under Cobb's picture is the speed. It's miles per hour."

"So that last pitch was ninety-seven miles per hour?" I asked. Papa nodded. "I've never even driven that fast."

"Now *that* is good to hear," Dad told me.

For the next pitch, I watched Cobb release it then checked the speed. Then I did it for every pitch after that.

In the seventh inning, Cobb was on the verge of walking a batter. Three balls, two strikes. Full count, as they say, but if he walked him, it would mean the other team got their first man on base. That wasn't great.

Cobb shook his head at Brooks three times, then Brooks's shoulder slumped for a second and Cobb nodded. He finally liked the pitch call that Brooks had made.

It was all going rather well, then Cobb released the ball.

I think every single person heard that ball hit the glove and then then ref said it was a strike.

When I glanced up at the scoreboard, the number I saw took my breath away.

"Holy shit." I leaned forward, then looked at Papa. "Did he really just throw that a hundred and one miles per hour?"

"He sure did." Papa grinned widely. "He had to get that batter out."

The music started up for the seventh inning stretch, but we didn't stand up.

"Looks like we've got a no-no going, Jonathan."

"It does."

"What's a no-no?" I asked. There were still so many terms that didn't make any sense to me. "What's a no-no?" They weren't answering me quick enough.

Papa leaned in close and whispered, "It's a no

hitter. But you're not supposed to talk about it or acknowledge it. It's bad luck."

I cocked my head to the side. "Like saying 'Macbeth' in a theater?"

"Exactly."

"But it's a big deal?"

"It's a *huge* deal," Dad told me. "They're not unheard of, but it's also not common. Most pitchers don't pitch full games so it's usually a combined one. As in, none of the pitchers allowed a hit. But I think Cobb's finishing this game."

"His pitch count is low," Papa added.

I sat back and listened to my dads debate over how the rest of the game was going to go and just how good my boyfriend was at what he did. But all I could think about was how good my boyfriend was going to be once we got back to his place.

In the top of the eighth inning, the batter tipped off back at Brooks. Brooks took off to catch it and slid into the railing of the other dugout. To me, it looked like his knee hit, but he caught the ball and hopped back up.

Then he took one step and hit the ground like someone had just unloaded a pile of bricks.

The Briggs men on the field took off running toward their brother. Urban got to him first, then

Cobb, then Silas. Even the short stop, Jenner Greene, skidded to a stop before running into him. Camden had told me that Jenner had been around since forever because he was Silas's best friend from when they'd been little. She'd rolled her eyes the entire time.

Cobb waved someone over and people surrounded Brooks.

"What happened?" I asked no one in particular.

"Looks like he got hurt," Dad said. "But how?"

"I think his knee hit the railing or the ground."

Suddenly, I couldn't remember what I'd seen. That was when I popped up from my seat and hurried down the aisle, passing in front of everyone else who was also on their feet. Then I went down the steps until I was near Camden. "Camden!" I called. She came over to me. "Is he hurt?"

She nodded. "Looks like it." Worry lined her face. "It's unusual because Brooks is never hurt. I mean, he gets bruised up, but never something to take him out of the game."

Before I could ask anything else, Cobb was under one of Brooks's arms and Silas under the other while Urban had his helmet and glove. They slowly made their way back to the dugout. Then everyone minus Brooks went back out onto the field and another catcher was at the plate.

Cobb threw a couple of practice pitches as I said, "What does this mean?"

"I don't know." Camden sighed. "It depends on what's hurt and how badly."

"Can I do anything?"

She shook her head. "They have the best doctors. Mom's probably already down there. He'll be all right."

"OK." I squeezed her arm. "Call me if anyone needs anything. I'm happy to help."

"Yeah." She took a deep breath. "You'll probably have to help Cobb later." Fighting a grin, she added, "No. Seriously. When a player gets hurt, it shakes them all. Reminds them of what can happen."

I smiled widely at her. "I'll do my best."

Then I returned to my dads.

Cobb did finish the game and it was a no-hitter just like Papa had predicted. They left after I assured them I was going out with Cobb tonight. All night? I mean... probably, but I didn't know yet.

At first, I was going to head downstairs, but then I saw Cobb come back out of the dugout and over to someone with a microphone. The on-field interview. After a no-hitter, that was a given, I suppose.

I made my way closer to where they were near third base. He was talking animatedly then caught me out of the corner of his eyes and smiled but focused back on the reporter.

When he was finished, he came over to me, but some other fans were hurrying toward us. "Meet me downstairs. I want to go check on Brooks."

"OK. I'll meet you down there."

I didn't hurry because it wasn't like Cobb would be there immediately. But once I'd gotten down there, I found a spot out of the way and sat on the floor to play on my phone. I'd taken some pictures during the game and decided that one I'd captured of him pitching was going to become my background.

Not knowing how much time had passed, I startled when he said, "Hey."

After jumping, I hopped up onto my feet and smiled. "How's Brooks?"

"He'll be all right." He reached out and took my had to lead me toward the door. "It's a muscle strain around the knee. He'll be out a little bit, but not forever." He pushed through the door to the outside.

"How long is 'a little bit'?"

"Normally, it'd be a few games, but we're going into the All-Star break, so he'll be out these two games, then five days off. Probably be back after that."

I stopped where I was. "You get five days off?"

He chuckled and gave me a tug. "No. Baseball does, but I'm playing in the All-Star game, as are my brothers, though not Brooks now."

There was still so much to learn.

We arrived at his car and he threw two bags into the back seat while I climbed into the passenger side. Then he got behind the wheel.

"Where is the game?" I asked because I hadn't looked it up in those short moments.

"Cincinnati."

I squeed, making him laugh again. "I could go, then, right? I mean, if tickets are available. That's an easy drive."

"Yeah. You can go. Camden's coming. My parents are coming." He groaned. "I'm sure they have a ticket, but that means being around my parents in the box."

I had to think about that. I hadn't met his mom or dad, only heard of then and his dad didn't sound pleasant. I'd make it work.

"Camden will be there. As I'm sure will Everly and Amity. You wouldn't be alone with them and I'll knock my dad out if he's a dick to you."

"I wouldn't want that," I countered. "I can handle dicks."

Cobbs loud laughter filled the car. "Oh, I know you can." I pushed him. That wasn't what I'd meant.

"Will Brooks be there?"

He shook his head. "He'll have to stay behind to rehab his knee." This was nice. It was easy. There was only one dark cloud still hanging over us. "I have some news, though." He reached out to caress my cheek. "I saw my mom when I checked on Brooks. She took me aside to let me know that the Hannah situation is over. My lawyer confronted her and her lawyer with some information the investigator got."

"They work quickly," I told him. I'd never been involved in anything like this so maybe it was normal and I just didn't know it.

"Yeah, well she confessed who the real father is and my mom got her dad to promise that they wouldn't bring me into their bullshit anymore."

I launched right into his arms, wrapping mine around his neck and squeezing. "Really?"

He held on to me tightly. It was awkward, given the position in the front seat of his car. "Really."

When I pulled back, the emergency brake digging into my knee, I asked, "So, who's the real father?"

He sighed. "I guess it's a friend of her dad's." I scrunched up my nose. "That's why she knew he'd be pissed."

"That's kind of gross."

"It is."

I worried my bottom lip between my teeth. "Does that mean you'll go back to New York?"

He ran a hand across my cheek. "No, Baby. I was traded here so I'll be staying here."

A satisfied smile appeared. "I have one more question," I said. He raised an eyebrow. "How quickly can you get us back to your apartment so we can finish what we started earlier and do you need to eat first? Okay, that's two questions."

His nostrils flared and he wet his bottom lip. "Put your seatbelt on because I can get us there pretty fucking quick."

I clapped my hands at the answer I'd wanted and slid back into my seat.

"And we'll order food later."

Before I could get my seatbelt on, Cobb

grabbed the back of my neck and pulled me to him then pressed his mouth to mine. His mouth was hot and demanding and pushing me to the point that I was about to climb into his lap again.

He rested his forehead against mine. "I fucking love you, Monroe."

The biggest grin spread across my face. "I love you, Cobb." Then I pulled back so he'd see that I was serious. "Now get us back to your place before I take advantage of you right here," I said. He snorted. "What? I'm needy."

A deep, sexy noise rumbled in his chest as he threw the car in reverse, pressing me against the seat. I pulled the seatbelt on right as he turned out of the parking garage.

I'd assumed meeting Cobb in that coffee shop was chance. Right now, I was starting to think that maybe it was fate.

I'd never given fate a second thought. Things happened. That was it.

But putting me there that day with Cobb was either fate or the best luck of my life.

BONUS SCENE

Dear Reader,

I hope you enjoyed Winning the Player. Cobb & Monroe were such fun for me to write. Monroe especially. Neither are in the best place to start a relationship, but…

I have a bonus scene for you as a thank you for reading. Just click the link below, sign up for my newsletter, and you'll get an email with the bonus scene.

SIGN UP HERE:
https://geni.us/Winning-Bonus

Meeting a hot baseball player at the courthouse wasn't on my bingo card.

Grabbing coffee after I was arrested—again—is a last minute decision. I know what I'm in for when I get home. Especially since this time, it's for something more than protesting. I've got more trouble than I know what to do with.

Now I'm going to find out what happens when you fall for someone who can't be with you. Trouble just keeps coming.

Winning the Player

He was my brother's best friend and off limits.

The world knows Silas Briggs as the baseball heartthrob on a hot streak. I know him as brother's former friend and my teenage crush.
Four years ago, he broke my young heart by making me think there could be something between us.

Then he left town and never looked back.

Now I'm back and working for the team, hoping that we can be friendly. Then I see him in person and friendship is the last thing on my mind.

START READING KISSING THE PLAYER TODAY

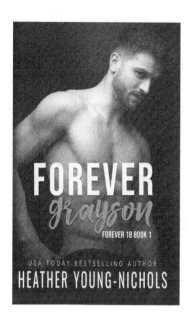

Do you love rock stars?

FOREVER GRAYSON

Forever 18 Book 1

One night three years ago is coming back to haunt me.

It was supposed to be one night then I'd never see him again. One night at a dive bar where I met someone who could scratch an itch.

He wasn't famous then.

Now he's a rock star.

A rock star whose manager just hired me to be the band's stylist. It's a dream job to me but it could be a nightmare.

Is it worse if he remembers me? Or worse if he doesn't?

START READING FOREVER GRAYSON NOW

Love your rock stars? Check out...
Daisy *Pushing Daisies Book 1*

Is it weird that I'm in a band with my brothers?
Not to me.

When I'm moved off our bus and onto the one that
belongs to the hot manager of the headlining band,
I know something's wrong.

Lawson is willing to take me on so some crazy fan
can't get to me but when things heat up... he backs
off. Says he's too old for me.

It's a small age gap. It doesn't mean a thing.

START READING DAISY NOW

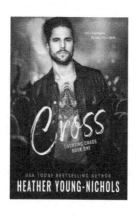

Cross *Courting Chaos Book 1*

When a sexy drummer mistakes me for a groupie and tries to kick me out of the venue, I'm willing to chalk it up to mistaken identity. Usually everyone knows me but I shouldn't assume. Now Cross wants to make it right ini the hope that my father won't kick his band off the tour.

In trying to make amends, Cross becomes my surprise protector when I accidentally snap some pictures of his bandmate in a bad situation and he wants them deleted.

Cross being my protector has me wanting something I've never wanted before… A sexy drummer.

Growing up with a famous father has taught me many things but the number one rule has always been NEVER FALL FOR A ROCK STAR.

I guess I want to break the rules.

START READING CROSS TODAY

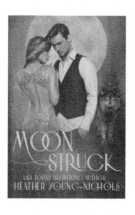

After living under my father's rule, I'm about to break free.

My father has kept me on a short leash my entire life.

The Orin comes for me.

Finding out what he is… scares the hell out of me.

Finding out I'm his supposed mate… I don't know that I'll recover.

START READING MOONSTRUCK TODAY

Being the daughter of my people's leaders, I should understand protocol and appropriate behavior. Problem is, I understand both, I just don't follow them.

But I have a different plan.

There's a boy... now a man, who is supposed to be powerful. I want him on our side.

What I didn't know is that together, he and I might be unstoppable.

Now I just have to find him.

START READING THE GREMLIN PRINCE TODAY

I'm a witch. Or so they tell me.

Finding out I'm a witch isn't even the weirdest part of my day. Having the guy who hated me in high school stand before me to tell me that I am, is.

Somehow, I'm supposed to learn spells and how to ground myself to the elements, fight the fact that I want him like I want air, and not freak out that my parents are part of a shadow coven trying to pull me over to the dark side.

Yeah. No problem.

START READING CURSED MAGIC TODAY

THE HARBOR POINT SERIES

A new adult contemporary romance series

Meet Gio and Sal.
Two damaged men who meet the woman who can set them right.

Then there's Cash.
He's not damaged but he's ready to do the healing when he meets Gemma.

START READING LOVE BY THE SLICE TODAY

THE FALLOUT SERIES

A new adult romance series

Coming home is hard.
Finding out the boy you loved had a baby with your
former best friend… heartbreaking.

START READING LAST GOOD THING TODAY

GAMBLING ON LOVE

A new adult romance series

Desperate times call for desperate measures so Flannery Tate is selling her virginity.

START READING HIGHEST BIDDER TODAY

I you'd like to just keep up with my sales and new releases, you can follow me on BookBub!

Bookbub: https://www.bookbub.com/authors/ heather-young-nichols

Heather Young-Nichols is a USA Today Bestselling author of contemporary and paranormal romances. She writes swoony heroes and snarky heroines with a heap of romance.

When she's not writing, she's binging a show with her kids, watching base-ball, or snuggling with her cuddly animals.

Find Heather on Social Media or by visiting her website.

heatheryoungnichols.com

f facebook.com/heatheryoungnicholsauthor

instagram.com/heatheryoungnichols

a amazon.com/Heather-Young-
Nichols/e/B00KKTM54A

BB bookbub.com/authors/heather-young-nichols

tiktok.com/@heatheryoungnichols

36562362R00218